For my mum – rest her soul.

"We are Angels, We are Demons
We are Children all the same."

Lyrics by **Jack Savoretti**

There are many, many, many worlds branching out at
each moment you become aware of your environment and
then make a choice."

Kevin Michel, Moving Through Parallel Worlds to
Achieve your Dreams.

Prologue

Glistening lemony light from a rising sun struggles to
filter through dense fog in ancient woodland. A spider
climbs a web covered in delicate droplets of dew which
accentuate the complexity of the arachnid's dragline silk.
Burnt orange and red leaves of a variety of shapes and
sizes are scattered along sparse snowy trails in the wood.
A red breasted robin flies nearby, almost flying into the
spider's' web; the little territorial bird swerves just in time
and lands on a small desolate branch to regard its
surroundings.

Sunlight filters through strongly now and the thick mist
begins to lift. The robin suddenly takes off, startled by
movement coming from a shrub close by. Something

appears to be moving, perhaps hiding. Further on in the distance there is whispering.

'He must be here somewhere.' A man whispers.

'He is.' Another man responds.

'Just come out mate, we won't hurt you and there is nowhere for you to run to anyway.'

Both men are wearing a dark hoodie and tracksuit bottoms and wellies, as if in some kind of uniform. One of the men wears a moustache and his jawline is chiselled, old marks are visible on his forehead from where he has bumped it several times on numerous door frames. He has never flown in a plane otherwise he would be sure to ask for extra leg room.

The other man looks more effeminate without any hair on his face and is shorter by two foot. They are both somewhat chubby in stature.

'For fucks sake just come out!' The taller guy bellows this time. 'You aren't going anywhere and it's cold and you must be starving now.'

'Yes.' The effeminate guy agrees. 'You've been out here all night, it's cold, wet and miserable and you must want something to eat.' He gapes at his colleague with an awkward smile.

A crow caws in the distance, a haunting sound as it lasts longer than expected. Another shuffling noise comes from somewhere nearby and both men peer at a bush of cotoneaster and blackberry laden with fruit.

The man with the moustache bends down on one knee and gazes intently at the bush. A tearful bloodshot eye widens in the undergrowth. The man reaches his hand through the thicket then yelps while withdrawing his hand quickly. He frantically picks at a few thorns embedded in his palm, whilst continuing to stare at the shrub. He slowly makes out an outline of a scratched bloody face in the thicket.

'Now, now, there's a good pal. Come out and let's go get something to eat and get you warm.' The partly concealed eye in the shrub blinks and a tear wells up and slowly runs down the side of his cheek. Both men close in on the shrubbery much more carefully this time.

Chapter 1

5 months later

In a spacious apartment similar to a studio flat a deep voice can be heard. In a window the London bridge can be seen in the distance. One side of the wall is bricked and supports a big painting of a village in fog; the fog surrounds the base of the village and both village and fog are surrounded by an intense foreboding black. The painting creates the illusion of a village suspended on a cloud enveloped in a dark abyss.

Two oversized windows fill the main wall and are furnished with silk white curtains and a roll up blind. The wall resembles that in a French urbane apartment. The colour of the wall is tangerine which blends in well with the Terracotta bricks on the side wall. Through this living room which comprises a ginormous white sofa and black wooden furnishings, is a kitchen with a huge island in the middle of a tiled floor, several utensils hang down over the island.

The island is burnt orange with cupboards on all sides and different coloured stools arranged next to it. A sizeable cooker boldly makes a focal point, it mimics a modern Aga. It is a dark green colour and an old fashioned kettle quietly whistles on a naked flame. Further down the apartment is a small hallway leading to a bedroom – a male voice resonates more clearly now and it is clear he is conversing on the phone with someone.

In the bedroom is a double bed slightly off the middle of the room and more silk white curtains, this time they are wavering in a light breeze coming in through the window. The walls are a shade of purple and host small framed pictures of two men. All the frames are of different colours, shapes and styles and are haphazardly placed on the wall creating a mosaic. The pictures are of two men in a tight embrace and in a couple they are kissing.

In the corner of the room is a small desk with a chair and on the other side of the wall a bookcase made of oak and filled with books. Most are self-help paperbacks, with a few on history and the practices of witchcraft and voodoo in the Tahiti islands. Through the bedroom is an ensuite painted in apple green and with a stylised sink, shower room and a separate oval bath next to a wall with an opening, like the kind of opening in an abode of an old Japanese movie – which opens to the bedroom.

The guy on the phone speaks with some intensity now; his face is half covered in shaving foam. Bushy eyebrows boldly take stance over his dark brown eyes. The eyebrows match his wispy cut dark brown hair. He resembles Colin Farrell.

'I do not want to hear anymore about it Grace – I know you mean well but I can't just sit around and wait for the police to handle this.' He leans in on the phone which is on loudspeaker by the sink.

'For all we know they are not even taking it seriously, just another homophobic police officer on the case. I have to go to this village myself to see if I can find any clues.' He scans his reflection in the mirror.

'He could have left his journal at a bed and breakfast or something – there must be some lead, something, I can't understand how he can disappear off the face of the earth!' He pauses, takes a breath, and looks at a yellow note on a side mirror which has been attached with a fancy magnet – it simple reads 'To Peter, my better half - flush the goddamn toilet! Love always Jaime.' Peter touches the note ever so slightly and a tear wells up in his left eye and trickles down his cheek.

'Okay Grace, I know, I will be careful I promise and I will text and facetime you at every opportunity, just so long as you don't pick on me for not shaving as I aim on letting my beard grow – one less thing to do whilst carrying out my own investigation.' He listens to Grace whilst still looking at the note on the mirror.

Peter is the eldest of four and he was always the black sheep of the family. He was the only one to attend University and albeit this was borne out of his desire to escape. He felt that his siblings were envious and resented him because of it.

He had an unhappy childhood, his father was abusive and mother was emotionally detached. So any chance he got he escaped into a book and hence honed his intellect and reading skills.

Peter never believed love was possible for him as he was incapable of flirting and small talk, he could not help but find it lame. He had no clue how to orchestrate the dating ritual. He did not get mind games and he was more the 'what you saw was what you got' kind of guy. This coupled with an abandonment issue over his mum meant that he found it extremely difficult when dating and actually dreaded it. For a long time he had given up on bothering. He believed dating applications were soul destroying and the bacchanalian nightlife tedious and so made a promise to himself to not bother and just put all his energy into his work and hobbies and friends.

That was until he met Jaime. Peter was in the library one hot afternoon. Most people would not have chosen to go to a library when the sun was out especially not in England. Any chance to get some heat you took it! Jaime had his head lost in a book he was reading whilst walking down an aisle. He walked straight into Peter and that was that.

'Okay I gotta finish the last of my packing. You look after yourself too and don't let Gavin treat you the way he does, you deserve better you know that.' He smiles whilst wiping away the tear that has trickled down his unshaven cheek. 'Goodbye.' He hangs up the phone. He finishes with his shaving on the right side of his face – 'the last time for a while whiskers.' He mutters to his reflection in the mirror.

He picks up the sticker from the mirror, grabs a towel and fastens it around his waist whilst walking into the bedroom. He ambles over to the bookcase, examines the top and pulls out a book, opening it up to the back where it reads *'Jaime Coombs, writer and researcher of the paranormal.'* A black and white picture is to the right of the page and right below are acknowledgements. Peter stares at his partner longingly whilst he sits on the bed.

Jaime was an adopted third child of his foster parents, it was rumoured he was found wandering alone in the woods when he was only five years old with no memory of what had happened. Jaime's guardians took him into their home when he was six years old.

He is a strongly opinionated character and prefers to be upfront about things. He does not like bullshit and admires people that are blunt. He gets on particularly well with autistic people. He's always excelled in writing and creating a world outside of his own- honed as a means to escape from a traumatic childhood where he had to watch his brother die from a genetic condition that slowly sucked the life out of him.

Jaime felt that his father made things worse as he was over sensitive about it and this impacted on Jaime's anxiety a lot. Writing became cathartic for him. He had accepted a life of solitude with one or two friends as he felt that he was incapable of being in love with someone due to his anxiety disorder. That was until he bumped into Peter in a library.

Peter sticks the note from the bathroom onto the side of the picture in the book. The snapshot reveals a man with designer stubble that accentuates a defined chin. He shows off short dark brown hair, mysterious dark eyes and a cheeky smile. He wears a smart deep purple shirt and a white tie. Peter wells up again and he wipes his eyes with his hand and closes the book entitled 'Exploring the magic of the world.' He places the hardback in his almost packed small suitcase and gets up to throw some clothes on. He shuffles over to the wardrobe and fishes out a pair of jeans, shirt and a jumper. A piercing whistling sound travels at him with increasing resonance.

'Damn it!' He rushes out to the kitchen where a ferocious kettle is bellowing out steam; he whips it off the stove and turns the cooker off. Hardly any water is left in it and he tuts to himself; he stomps over to the fridge, opens it and grabs a bottle of orange juice. 'Costa it is then.' He slams the fridge door shut. He considers the time on his phone whilst walking back to the bedroom, maintaining the annoyance in each step.

Chapter 2

Peter looks out the window of a train as it hurdles up a hill into mountains and countryside. The scenery is breathtakingly serene and he wonders why he has never ventured to these parts before. It reminds him of areas in North Wales on a sunny day, sunshine being rare in those parts of the UK. Albeit with climate change he doubted this would continue. Bright and rapidly moving clouds in the wind create shadows that meander over the countryside like angelic phantoms caressing nature.

'Clophill our next and final stop.' A voice comes through the intercom – it crackles just towards the end of the message. Peter checks his mobile phone and smiles.

'Just in time.' He stands up, grabs his suitcase from the carriage above and checks his pockets – he has formed this habit before disembarking any vehicle. He feels for his wallet and phone before setting off. He struts to the exit of the train and steps off.

"How refreshing it is not to hear 'Please mind the gap' as is often heard when in the London underground. He makes his way to the exit of the station then saunters to the taxi rank where he's pulled towards a yellow taxi. It reminds him of his stay in New York City. He enters the taxi, instructing the driver to please take him to the Dragons Inn. The driver takes a look at him and pauses for a brief moment before saying, 'Fine – that will be about £7.89p.' Peter nods his head and smiles and cannot help wondering how come the driver is so exact with the amount.

The taxi pulls away from the train station and makes its way onto an A road. Meanwhile Peter checks his mobile phone for any messages. He was having problems getting a signal whilst on the train and for some bizarre reason he was unable to get onto the so called free Wi-Fi. As soon as he had pulled his phone out of his pocket it buzzes alerting him to three texts. One is from Grace – and plainly reads *'Hope you got there in one piece?'* Peter decides to ignore this text for the time being as he is expecting to hear from a detective that he's found to help him in his search for his missing partner. The private investigator is gay; his hope is that the guy would be more sympathetic to the predicament he is in. He does think to himself how silly that he has to hire a gay detective but despite being in the 21st century; society was still infused with homophobia - dripping with it!

A text from the detective reads – *'Meet you at the Dragons Inn at 6pm, Ryan.'* He checks the time and its past 4pm. "Should be just enough time."

The other is a message from the 'PPI' people; he deletes the text and wonders when they will put something in place to prevent all cold calls and texts. He then returns to the message from Grace and responds - *'Just arrived at Clophill and now in a cab on way to the Inn X.'* He types quickly and he looks up to notice that the driver is looking at him through the rear mirror. The driver keeps his stare for a brief moment which for some reason causes a slight shiver to creep up Peter's neck. The driver eventually returns his attention to his driving.

'First time in these parts sir?'

'Erm, yes it is.' Peter continues to look at the rear mirror expecting the driver to return his stare, but he doesn't, he merely responds with a mumble and nods his head. As the taxi continues up a back road, Peter peers out the window and notices all the houses are made of brick similar to the terracotta bricks on the wall in his living room. He wonders if Jaime noticed this too when he arrived here. He also notices how deserted the village looks; no one is about - the odd car but not a soul to be seen crossing the road or walking around. The only thing missing was tumbleweed.

'Is it always this quiet?'

'Oh, there's a town meeting this evening I'spose everyone's at that. It's a very strong community here; everyone looks out for each other if you know what I mean.' This time the driver looks at the rear mirror, and Peter stares back at a deadpan face.

'I – I see.' Peter manages to expel.

'I'm assuming there will be people at the Inn to check me in?' Peter attempts to break the ice, as he feels a little awkward to say the least and the driver peers at the rear mirror again with the same expressionless face.

'Yea there'll be someone to see you get settled in alright.' He keeps his stare for a while before returning to concentrate on the road. The town is so deserted he doesn't have to concentrate that much.

A few minutes pass and the yellow taxi pulls up at a petrol station. This time the driver turns round to speak.

'I'll just be a minute, need to collect something from ere.'

'Oh……..Okay.' He can't understand why he feels intimidated by this driver. He is a highly respected financial analyst in the city of London for God's sake, and here he is in the back of a taxi with as little self-confidence as a young school girl with dire taste in ponytail ribbons!

"And this is weird – a taxi driver stopping to do his own business when there is a passenger?! What is that all about?" He decides to pick up the courage to address the driver about this when he returns.

Peter peers out the side window; a sign with the words 'Pit Stop' in dark red letters is strategically positioned so as to be seen from as many angles as possible. "American and kind of apt but unusual name nonetheless for a petrol station, at least it expresses its function clearly.

He scans further along inside the garage and watches the driver of the cab speaking to the guy at the till. Both men glance over at the stationary car, unflinchingly looking at Peter for a few unsettling seconds. Eventually, the driver taps the till operator on his shoulder and makes to exit the garage. He slumps back to the cab, which reinforces Peter's decision to talk to the driver about the inappropriate pit stop! As the driver slides into the vehicle he immediately turns round to Peter making Peter jump in his seat.

'I'm sorry about that, had to get directions, needed to make sure was taking you to the right Inn.'

'Is there more than one Dragons Inn?' Peter fidgets in his seat.

'There is actually.' The driver announces.

'There's more than one Dragons Inn in a small town?' Peters emphasises every word.

'Yes I'm afraid so.' The driver remarks without checking Peter's reflection.

The cab pulls away from the petrol station and turns onto a dirt road.

Chapter 3

The taxi arrives at a big house with a large swinging sign at the side with the words 'Dragons Inn'. Sudden darkness from cumulonimbus clouds engulf outside and a persistent breeze sways the branches of the trees around. Peter thanks the cab driver whilst giving him money; he decides not to give him a tip as he collects the change.

"If I couldn't pick up the courage to speak to you about stopping at a garage because you have no sense of direction, I'm sure as hell not giving you a tip."

He takes hold of his small suitcase and automatically abiding to his routine of checking his pockets, he gets out of the taxi.

'Thanks again.' Peter shuts the door of the taxi and the driver nods with no visual acknowledgment. Peter struts off towards the pub. "Yes I did not give you a tip and that is my God given right." He approaches the door with a sign that reads "free house" he remembers laughing at this description in the past as there was nothing free about it. He later found out it meant that it wasn't controlled by a brewery and so not restricted to selling any kind of alcohol. As he reaches for the door handle the breeze stops and the sign stops swinging. He tries not to give in to the anxiety being induced from the events so far.

He enters the Inn and is instantly hit by a distinctive aroma; like Marzipan with a clinical hint of formaldehyde. "At least it doesn't stink of unclean carpets masked by some ungodly smelling air freshener." He does wonder which of the smells is sicklier after a while of inhaling. He approaches the reception counter where someone sits. The man is concealed by the counter at first glance.

'Hello.' Peter announces in a forced cheery voice and the man who is sat down back to him turns around startled. The man appeared to be staring at a blank wall. Peter was sure he hadn't put down any reading material.

'Hello…...sorry did not hear you come in.'

The man is wearing a hoodie and tracksuit bottoms. He is a middle aged fellow with stubble and piercing blue eyes. Peter is taken aback by just how blue his eyes are. The greetings are interrupted by another man, this time a black man wearing a suit and wellies.

'All done.' The black man declares managing a smile. Light reflects off his shiny bald head which compliments his goatee and trimmed eyebrows. Peter wonders if the guy is gay. He remembers chatting and having a laugh with his partner about some gay men who are obsessed with trimming their eyebrows and how unattractive this was to them.

'I'm Mr Coleman; I booked a reservation over the phone.' Peter is aware the word reservation sounds American but he prefers this phrase to 'I have booked' or 'I have a booking here.' The man with the hoodie inspects the laptop suitably positioned on the desk so as to create space for a signing in book.

'Yes, here you are - It will be room three which is round the corner, past the fireplace to your right and up the small stair way and then left.' He hands Peter the key attached to a key ring with a huge number three which appears to be made of bone. It's like a chiselled instrument for the Australopithecus man! "With such a large key chain it makes it near impossible to lose the key I suppose."

'Thank you.' Peter acknowledges while reaching into his pocket and takes out a photograph of Jaime.

'Have you seen this man?' he does this without flinching. He has no idea where he's picked up the courage to do this. He certainly hadn't planned to – he just did it involuntarily and he points the picture to the man in the hoodie. The black man turns around to look also.

'No.' They both say in unison. 'I don't believe I have.' the man in the hoodie responds and turns back to his laptop. At that moment Peter's phone rings and he scrambles in his pocket for his phone and answers it straight away. It's the detective he's planned to meet at the Inn. 'Yes.' Peter answers smiling.

'I'm afraid there's been a problem.'

It's a little difficult to hear Ryan on the other end of the phone. The two guys at the reception desk reluctantly peel their eyes off what they are doing to look at Peter.

Chapter 4

A crackling noise replaces Ryan's voice and the call is eventually intercepted.

'Hello.' Peter knows full well he has been cut off. He detests this reaction in movies when the actor continually utters 'Hello, hello are you there?'- knowing full well that the phone has been cut off. Yet here he is doing the same thing. He chuckles to himself nervously, simultaneously checking his signal, he has one bar.

'Bad reception here then.' Peter mentions whilst regarding the man in the hoodie and again chuckles to himself as he realises the irony. Its bad reception all round.

'You should be okay out the front.' The black man states without turning round from a task he's gotten engrossed in.

Peter walks out to the front of the Inn where he came in, still clutching onto his small suitcase and his bedroom key.

He dials the number to the detective, whilst spotting the Dragons Inn sign has taken to swinging again, this time more powerfully and with a creaking noise. Peter observes his surroundings and senses a storm brewing.

'Hi Peter.' a voice on the other end of the mobile phone answers.

'Ryan, are you okay?' Peter strains his face to listen, attempting to cut out the sound of the wind and squeaking Inn sign.

"Why do people do that when trying to listen – contorting face muscles has nothing to do with helping you hear better but yet we do it."

The reception is not good at all. Peter wanders further away from the Inn.

'I'm afraid I'm going to be late – I am stuck in traffic, I think there's been an accident or something. I can see a fallen branch on the road and lots of lights. Bad storm coming in.' Ryan reports.

'I see....... Well no rush – get here when you get here but be careful. Heads up, the reception is not that good here, on the phone or otherwise. When you do arrive, call me before you come into the pub and I'll come down to the lobby, Okay?'

'Okay. hopefully not more than an hour.'

'Okay, see you soon, drive carefully.'

'Okay, bye.' The connection goes dead.

Back in the pub Peter passes the reception and recalls the directions to his room. He decides not to ask the two people at the desk again. He's not in the mood. He strolls past a stone fireplace crackling with fiery heat.

"A satisfying shot of brandy sitting next to that will be just lovely."

He walks further to the right and accidentally hits his suitcase on the corner wall. He mutters then continues and finds the small stairway, goes up it and bears left. Before doing so he peers out of a bay window at the top of the stairs. Two leafless and lifeless trees stand out in the distance like two skeletal alien twins embracing. The way they've grown mimic the arteries and veins of someone's lungs - upside down.

'Fractal patterns.' he mummers. Jaime used to talk about this, informing him on how all of nature was made up of replicated fractal patterns and it was consistent throughout. The veins in a leaf were almost identical to the branches of the tree and so on. It was referred to as the golden ratio in nature and the Fibonacci sequence, all demonstrating how living things have evolved to mimic one another. You could go as far as noticing that the neural network in the brain or eye was the same as a snapshot of the universe, but that was something else altogether.

He finds the number three on a door and opens it with the key he has been given. He saunters in and shuts the door gently behind him and turns around. The room is surprisingly decent, judging from the people he had encountered at the reception desk he would have expected the room to be quaintly furnished and uncouth, but on the contrary. The internal decoration throughout the room is tasteful. It has a good sized bed, which is nicely decorated with crisp white linen and two big puffed up pillows, without the excessive pretentious cushions you often got scattered all over a bed at a posh hotel. "You only had to go through the hassle of removing them before climbing into bed so what was the point?"

A desk and chair are propped up against a window, outside in the distance are the two skeletal trees that look like the x-ray of a pair of lungs.

He throws his suitcase on the bed and enters the bathroom – again clean and decent enough. He reaches the sink, turns the tap on and washes his face and hands using the sandalwood and vanilla soap provided. He grabs the towel and dabs his face with it. It's not too old or brand new either. He can't stand it when the towel is so new it rubs the water around your body without drying or when it's so overused that it's like giving yourself a body scrub with a loofah!

He ambles back into the bedroom and sits down on the bed to contemplate. Suddenly a bright flash casts detailed shadows across the room, he glimpses out the window and it is lightning. He waits for the sound of thunder and sure enough after a few moments there is the cacophony of a thousand atmospheric drums. He gets up and gazes at the dead trees and again there is another bolt of lightning. He takes his mobile phone out of his pocket and checks the signal, about half a bar fluctuates on the screen.

"The storm can't be helping."

He sits down at the desk and moves his hand against the side. He exclaims and curses whilst inspecting his hand. A splinter of wood has lodged itself into the palm of his hand. He removes it and sucks on his palm just in time for another lightning and thunder – this time they are a lot closer together.

"Right overhead."

He glances over to the right side of the desk, and is about to throw the wood splinter into a small waste bin provided and spots a crumpled piece of paper in it. He reaches for it, exchanging it for the splinter and opens it up.

"Own your suffering with joy, knowing that it is in that space your greatness resides." is written on the piece of paper and Peter scrutinises the note as he reads it again.

He walks over to his suitcase and fishes out the book written and published by his lover and opens it up. He finds the sticker that he had removed from the mirror in their apartment. He inspects the writing and then checks the note he has retrieved from the bin again. The prose is identical.

"Could Jaime have stayed in this very bedroom? What are the chances? And how come the crumpled note is in the bin despite the pristinely clean room?" He places the creased note with the sticker in the book just as another flash of lightning scatters light around his room and this time it's a while before the thunder follows.

"Moving over quite swiftly."

He checks the time on his phone; he hasn't owned a watch for a long time. He often wondered how the wristwatch industry still kept up business when you can get the time on any decent mobile phone. "I mean why be bothered with a watch – just another thing to clasp to and be mindful of. It's only a matter of time before they are completely out of business just like 'TomTom or Sat Navs are becoming. When you can own a very good Google mapping app on your phone why bother with purchasing a Sat Nav? Funny how times change."

He gets up from the desk and starts to unpack his suitcase. He picks out his neatly folded clothing and walks over to the wardrobe which is a fair sized mahogany furniture with handles shaped like horseshoes. He opens it up and for a second is alerted to the whiff of his lover's aftershave. He always wore Joop and Peter loved the scent especially when he was kissing his neck. Peter moves closer to the clothes cabinet, almost walking into it and he sniffs deeply and again the faint aroma of Joop. He continues to draw in breathe through his nose and savours the fragrance and the moment.

"Could it be my imagination?"

He remembers reading somewhere that imagination can be so powerful as to activate sensory perceptions like smell and even sight. Is he going to be seeing an apparition of his lover sitting on the bed admiring him? Or could he have been in this exact room? What are the chances?

A tear wells up in his left eye, always his left eye to start when feeling emotional. Why he wonders to himself, trying to distract himself as he wipes the tear that is now running down the side of his face. A knock on the door startles him, more because it happens in unison with another thunder. Had there been a previous knock concealed by the storm? He's not sure but he walks over to the door and reaches for the handle and opens the door.

Stood before him is the guy from reception.

'Everything to your satisfaction sir?'

'Y- Yes, thank you……..very good.' Peter smiles hoping the receptionist does not notice his emotional moment.

'Great.' utters the man with piercing blue eyes. 'If you need anything please just lift up the phone that is by your bed.' The man is about to leave when Peter puts his hand in his pocket again and shows him the picture of Jaime.

'You're certain you haven't seen this man?' Peter presents the picture.

'I can't say that I have…….Who is he?'

'Oh………. a very dear friend.' Peter replies. "No need to test homophobia in this small town."

'Do you want me to put a copy of the picture downstairs to see if anyone recognises him?'

Really kind – but maybe later.' For some reason he does not feel comfortable with this idea.

'Okay, well as I say, phone's over there if you need anything.' He points to the receiver by the bedside and smiles revealing yellow teeth. "Europeans don't quite care for pristine white teeth like the Americans do but there is no need to have your teeth that yellow!"

'Thank you......thank you very much, appreciate it.' "Such a shame, perfect blue eyes with yellow teeth."

The man turns to leave, but Peter remembers something.

'Oh I'm expecting a friend, he might be here any minute – he will ask for me. I told him to call or text me when he's near the Inn but being as the signal is not that great.' He purposely chooses the word signal over the word reception this time. 'He may not be able to get hold of me. Actually do you have Wifi?'

'Yes we do as a matter of fact, here's the passcode.' He hands Peter a card.

'Thanks.' Peter acknowledges, wondering if the man will see the difference between their teeth.

'I will call for you when your visitor arrives.' The man smiles again revealing his yellow gnashers and he leaves closing the door behind him gently.

"He can't have noticed the difference in our teeth as he willingly flashed his yellow teeth at me again, well at least he doesn't have plucked eyebrows."

Another flash of lighting scatters dark defined shadows across the room and this time it is a long while before the thunder follows.

"Certainly moving away as fast as it came. Never known a storm to come and go so quickly."

He goes back to the desk and sits down, checking his palm, a little blood seeps out and he sucks on his palm again. He peeks at his phone which now has a full bar of signal.

"Hopefully Ryan should have enough to text me when he's here."

He decides to text Grace using Whatsapp. He uses the card the receptionist gave him and enters the Wifi passcode on to his phone.

"Should have thought of this before but then Ryan would not be able to use Whatsapp until getting here so."

He waits for his phone to register the Wifi at the pub and then sends a text.

'Hi, arrived at the Inn. Very nice Inn but strange staff with custard yellow teeth.'

As he presses send, his phone beeps with another text from Ryan.

'I might be a little longer as I think I've arrived at another Inn which also happens to be called Dragons Inn. Grrrrrrr.'

"So the taxi driver wasn't joking when he said there were several Inns with the same name, not sure why I would think he was joking he certainly didn't seem the type to make jest. What on Earth would make a small town have Inns with the same name?"

'Okay how long do you think you'll be?'

'Another hour I think.'

'Okay.' Peter puts his phone on the desk.

Thankfully he has curbed the impatience he feels with people being late. It used to drive him crazy when people weren't on time, but he had to learn to let go of this. As it used to make him mad with anger, and he realised that the universe has a funny way of repeatedly throwing things at you that you have an issue with. So it was simple, he either let go of his obsession with time and lateness or persistently remain in a state of anger because despite the best intentions, people were people and some of them had a different relationship with time.

He gets a whiff of Joop again and turns around in his chair to examine the wardrobe. He is convinced now that Jaime stayed at this Inn – in this very room. "But why had the receptionist not seen him? Perhaps the receptionist was new to the role. I should have asked how long they had worked at the Inn to be sure." Until you ask the question straight out he had learnt not to make assumptions.

"I'm not making a very good investigator so far."

Chapter 5

Peter walks around in ancient woodland. A stony church stands a few yards away. He strolls over to the place of worship trying to avoid getting stung by Nettles. He scans the area for Dock leaves just in case. He hears a baby crying in the distance.

He arrives at the chapel grounds which is a graveyard with tombstones arranged all around the church.

"Strange."

The sound of the baby crying becomes clearer and sounds muffled.

The crying appears to be coming from a particular tombstone. Peter approaches it and bends down to inspect the engraving. "Jaime Coombs – loved and cherished by Peter Coleman." is etched in bold letters. A word is partly concealed by Bramble. He can make out the capital letter B.

He attempts to clear the bramble, carefully to avoid getting scratched. The sound of the muffled crying intensifies now.

The word is Bac ꝏ – the word does not make sense. "The letter at the end is strange, is it an old ancient letter?"

A mound of earth moves by the tombstone and Peter tries to clear the soil with his hands – The crying continues. There is more movement and Peter hurriedly moves soil to reveal what is underneath. Something pushes from under the soil. A baby's arm unearths. Now the crying is ear piercing, as a baby's dirty face is revealed, maggots squirm around in the eye sockets of a partly decomposed head.

Peter awakens with a jolt – he had fallen asleep on the desk. He can hear a cat meowing in the distance. It is one of those haunting meows which sound eerily like a baby crying.

'Jeez.' He mutters to himself as he pushes himself off the desk. He wonders why such a strange dream. He does not normally have such vivid dreams and this one in particular was creepy as hell. He checks his phone, two missed calls. 'Damn it.' He realises the missed calls are from Ryan. He presses dial on the number showing on his phone and gets up to walk to the window to search for the meowing cat.

'Yes, hello…. Sorry I missed your call.' Peter apologies with a sense of relief. 'I fell asleep in my room – must be all the travelling, it's drained me.' A brief pause. 'You are downstairs in the lobby now?' A pause. 'Okay I'll come straight down.' He hangs up the phone and grabs his partner's book taking it with him out the room.

Downstairs Ryan is sitting by the fire – just where he would have sat after coming in from a storm.

'Thank you so much for coming to meet me.' Peter hands out his hand for a shake.

'A pleasure.' Ryan stands up to shake his hand and then sits back down. 'I'm having a brandy, you want one?'

'I will get these.' Peter boasts and struts to the bar and orders a couple glasses of brandy. Three other people in the bar chat away in a civilised fashion; they temporarily eye him up and down and then return to their conversation.

Peter returns to the fire place with the two glasses of brandy in one hand; he adroitly hands over a glass to Ryan whilst still holding onto his glass.

'So... You made it?' Peter remarks with a smile as he sits down.

'Just about…...it was a strange situation. Someone had lost control of their car and ploughed into a small bridge barrier. The scene was cordoned off. But the car was still intact, apart from a small dent. It hardly seemed fatal but it was being treated as a horrific accident. It didn't make sense.'

'Hmmmm, that is strange.'

'Yes it was….anyway let's return to the matter at hand shall we?'

'Yes, of course, well the last time I heard from Jaime he was onto something. He said that he may have discovered something strange about this town or village.'

'Oh.' Ryan pays undivided attention.

'Yes, as I told you he was researching witchcraft.'

'Okay.' Ryan tries to keep his facial expression as nonchalant as possible.

'Yes he was fascinated about it and more so because there was some history here that dates back to the medieval times.'

'I see.' Ryan pulls out his notepad from his jacket pocket.

'I managed to get hold of a white witch who Jaime had gotten in touch with whilst he was here. She had helped him out with some information, and they met a couple of times. I figured she might know something about his whereabouts just before he... erm disappeared.' Peter firmly holds the book his partner has written.

'So you think we should start there?'

'I do.'

'How about information from the police, what have they got so far?'

'Well not that much which is why I contacted you. They're under the impression Jaime found another lover and wanted out of our relationship. Of course that is absurd.' Peters scoffs defiantly.

'You sound very sure.'

'That's because I am - No way he left me. We were like soul mates and even if he wanted out, he would never have done it without speaking to me about it first. We were friends first and foremost. I refuse to believe that is what happened and I resent the police for belittling our relationship in such a way.'

'Okay, I hear you.' Ryan pleads. 'I just need to be clear that that option is eliminated. You understand?' Ryan writes "We were like soul mates" in his pad and sympathises with Peter for not saying "We ARE like soul mates." instead.

'Yea, I do – The police are focussing on woodland nearby and they have scouted the wood for any signs but cannot find anything.'

'Okay well that is somewhere we can start then.' Ryan claims.

'I do prefer it if we meet with Contiana first.' Peter advocates.

'Contiana?'

'Oh…..the white witch, that's her name.'

'Hmmm funny name…..okay well we can do that first thing tomorrow morning I'm guessing you've arranged it with her?'

'Yes I have and she is looking forward to seeing us, she sounded quite genial. She has a lovely cottage in the woodland.'

'Would you like anything else to drink?' The barman interrupts. 'We'll be closing soon.' The barman is red haired and owns unusually large hands and feet. He stands about six feet and has a distinctive jaw line that somehow complements his immense hands and feet. His eyes are piercing blue and are somewhat sullen in appearance. He is less weird than the receptionists. Peter thinks to himself.

'Oh okay yea – could we have another couple of brandies please. I've got these Peter.' Ryan conveys with a smile.

As the barman shuffles off Peter returns his focus on Ryan. 'By the way what did you think about the people at the reception?'

'What about them?'

'Well, didn't you think they were somewhat strange?'

'No, not really.'

'Well they both had wellies on and acted bizarre; one of the guys had unusually yellow teeth.'

'Guys you say?'

'Yes there were two men – one white and the other black. They seemed out of place somehow.'

'Perhaps they were out of place.'

'What'dya mean?'

'Well women greeted me at the reception when I arrived – two beautiful women, both white and they seemed very pleasant and receptive.'

'Oh……..that's weird. There were two men when I came in. Perhaps they were on another shift and were replaced by the ladies before you arrived.' Peter holds his partners book tightly to his stomach.

'That must be it.' Ryan takes a big swig of his brandy.

'So are you staying at this inn too?'

'No, no I'm staying with an old friend who lives in these parts, I haven't seen her for a while so I might as well stay with her – she only lives in the neighbouring village some twenty five minutes' drive away.'

'Oh okay.' Peter wishes Ryan was staying in the Inn, he would have felt a lot more secure.

'Will you be okay driving?' Peter observes his empty glass.

'I'll get a cab. I'll be back here tomorrow to get my car and will drive to Contiana's if you like?'

'That will be lovely – thank you.' Peter replies and gulps the last of his brandy whilst getting up to escort Ryan to the door. It is now 11:45pm – funny how time flies especially when engrossed in something, whatever that something is, even witchcraft hunts.

Chapter 6

Peter is walking in a cemetery – Dense fog engulfs the ground and a faint sound of a crying baby resonates. The thick mist swirls around Peter's legs as he saunters through the grave stones. The crying begins to intensify and Peter is now alarmed. He stops suddenly and declares out loud. 'This is just a dream and I do not wish to be here anymore.' He closes his eyes whilst demanding to wake up, but doesn't.

"Funny how sometimes you have control and can forcefully wake up from an unpleasant dream and other times the thought does not cross your mind that you can wake up."

Something drops near his feet; he opens his eyes hesitantly, focussing at where his feet would be were they not immersed in dense fog. He slowly lifts his right foot and starts to shake it, attempting to clear the fog. Whimpering echoes around him and he bends down to focus through the fog whilst still waving his foot around. He can just about make out what appears to be a baby's head, the way it is positioned suggests he is standing over the body of the baby so he frantically steps back. Mewling din continues to reverberate and he crouches further to focus on the ground, this time waving his hand slightly to clear the fog. He puts his hand to his mouth to stifle a scream. The head is not attached to a body at all. In that moment of realisation its eyes open and just as Peter gasps in shock the head speaks in a mature voice. 'This is no dream – this is very much real.' and with that the infant's head screams.

Peter wakes up and sits up in bed and allows his brain to reconfigure. He has a weird feeling; he checks his phone, it is past 7am. For all accounts he has had a good night's sleep, despite the haunting dream yet again of a cemetery and crying baby. He jolts out of bed. He has gotten into the habit of doing this as he wakes up, as otherwise his thoughts take over and he is prone to overthinking, often negatively. He heads for the bathroom in his shorts, scratching his stomach the entire way. Despite the unpleasant dream he has an erection which is visible through his shorts. He now marches to the bathroom with more urgency. He stands over the toilet and urinates whilst thinking about the dream.

"Why a cemetery and why the crying baby? Is it some kind of premonition?"

He shakes both big head and little head simultaneously then shambles over to the sink to wash his face. He uses the little bar of lavender soap on the sink. Afterwards he grabs his toothbrush and squeezes some Euthymol toothpaste on it, puts it under the tap, wetting the bristles slightly and starts to brush his teeth. He becomes present to the brushing, mindfully, something he started doing after reading the book called NOW. He focuses on nothing but brushing his teeth, admiring himself in the mirror and being fully conscious to his dental hygiene. He rapidly turns around dropping his shorts again and squeezes more urine out whilst still brushing.

"Why does no one tell you about these things that happen to you as you age? Reserved wee from nowhere."

For some reason whilst brushing his teeth he always has that little bit more pee reserved for a running tap. He pulls on his penis attempting to squeeze out every last drop. He has learnt not to shake it as droplets of urine go everywhere, mostly on the walls. His partner had nagged him about this and literally showed him what to do by taking his partner's penis in his hand and slowly pulling and squeezing, much like what you would do when milking a cow. Peter smiles at his reflection in the mirror as he continues brushing his teeth. A tear wells up in his eye and coincides with a semi erection.

Peter's phone vibrates on the side table by the bed and he struts over to it, knowing it must be Ryan calling to say he is on his way or indeed is already in the lobby waiting. He picks up his phone.

'On my way – just leaving now.'

Peter puts the phone down and strides back to the bathroom, enters and shuts the door.

The bathroom door opens after a few minutes and a lot of steam bellows out of the bathroom with him, almost like the fog in his dream. He hurries out of the steamed bathroom perhaps subconsciously aware of what it is reminding him of and he opens the wardrobe.

"What do you wear to go visit a white witch?"

He stands naked staring at the clothes as water droplets take delight in caressing down his manly physique. He eventually pulls out a clean pair of jeans and a dark purple t-shirt and then puts some socks on and his comfortable walking shoes. He grabs his phone and hurriedly texts back.

'I will be downstairs in the lobby waiting for you – If you don't see me I may still be in the breakfast bar.'

Down the stairs Peter meets with the receptionist – this time it is the same guy with the bird's eye custard yellow teeth.

'Good morning Sir.' He flashes his teeth at him. 'Hope you had a good night sleep. Breakfast is being served if you would like to make your way to the breakfast bar to your left.'

'Yes – thank you.' Peter tries to avoid staring at his teeth. He is partly pleased this guy is back working so he can point him out to Ryan when he arrives and affirm he was not making it all up. With the dreams he's been having he wants to be clear of his reality.

He strolls left and into a small quaint dining area which displays a good spread of yoghurt, fruit, cereal, toast, croissants and eggs. He helps himself to some fruit and yoghurt which he places in one bowl and then scoopers up some scrambled eggs and picks two slices of toast which he puts on a separate plate. He goes to sit at a spare table for two but not before picking up a newspaper. He does this by adroitly placing the plate of scrambled eggs and toast in his right hand which is also carrying the bowl of fruit and yoghurt and he picks the newspaper up with his left hand.

He sits down and the chair creaks, he peeks around to see if anyone had detected this but no one appears to have noticed. He wiggles in the chair, testing the stability; the last thing he needs is to fall off his chair covered in yoghurt and scrambled eggs!

He delicately places both dishes on the table just as a waitress pours him a cup of coffee. 'Thank you.' Peter acknowledges ensuring to make eye contact with the waitress. He made a point of doing this as it angers him when people don't properly acknowledge people who are serving them – it's plain rude.

He opens the newspaper and an article jumps out at him:

STRANGE MOTOR ACCIDENT ON 'A' ROAD

Peter homes in to read the article as he is sure it is the accident that Ryan was referring to yesterday. On reading further, it reports the driver had an unfortunate aneurysm which caused him to crash into a post – he died before impact. Peter studies the picture of the car that is with the article; he spots a sign which has the word "cemetery" on it.

Peter's phone vibrates in his pocket which startles him a little.

'I am here'.

'Come into the restaurant.' Peter texts back.

As soon as he presses send, Ryan walks into the restaurant also holding the same newspaper Peter is reading.

'Oh you saw it then.' Ryan mutters as he sits down.

'Yes, but nothing about it appears strange from what I've read so far.' Peter declares.

'Well it states aneurysm but I'm not too sure.' Ryan interjects.

'What are you insinuating, that the papers made up a cover story?'

'From what I could see as I drove past – the guy looked dried up.'

'What do you mean – dried up?'

'Well…..you know….. like he'd been dead for some time.'

'Don't be ridiculous.' Peter finally responds after a brief pause.

'Perhaps I was imagining it – so when is Contiana expecting us?' Ryan regards the still uneaten breakfast in front of Peter.

'Oh not till 9am – checked it on Google map and it should take us little less than 40 minutes, pending on the traffic of course.' Peter hurries his toast and eggs down him.

'By the way did you see the lads at the reception desk like I was telling you about when I first arrived?' Peter is careful not to have eggs and toast fall out of his mouth as he speaks.

'You are kidding right.'

'No I am not kidding, one of the guys showed me to the breakfast room when I came down.'

'Well I hate to disappoint you but there were the same two ladies I saw when I arrived yesterday - no men at the reception I'm afraid.'

Peter stares at him like a startled rabbit on a busy road at night; some partly eaten scrambled eggs can be seen in his gaping mouth.

'You did not see a man with yellow teeth at the reception when you came in?' Peter tries to swallow his eggs.

'No I'm afraid I didn't.'

Peter rises and marches to the reception where he finds to his disbelief two young ladies just as Ryan had said. He stands still staring at the floor for a few moments then turns around to walk back to the restaurant but halts again, glimpses at the floor for a couple of seconds and walks right up to the ladies and shows them the picture of Jaime.

Chapter 7

Both Peter and Ryan are in a car, Ryan is driving. The car which is a grey classic Chevrolet and seems looked after, whizzes down country lanes surrounded by woodland.

'I don't understand, how could there be blokes one minute then women the next?' Peter stares intently at the road.

'Perhaps they have a tight shift and they happen to make the shift change when you've been around.' Ryan suggests turning to Peter momentarily.

'They didn't recognise Jaime either.' Peter mumbles.

'It's likely nothing, stop over analysing. So this lady....Contiana, where did you find her again?' Ryan turns his attention back to the road.

'Well Jaime and I met her at a witch convention round about the time Jaime started his research on his book. She seemed a nice enough lady, genial like you would expect a hippie to be. I had never met a white witch before and had no idea about them and what in fact the difference was. I remember being that ignorant about it; I asked if there were colour codes for different powers or something like that.'

'I see.....'

Suddenly a big jolt rocks them all in the car. The jolt causes Peter to hit his head on the headliner of the car, thanks to the automotive headlining it doesn't hurt. Ryan pulls over into a lay-by, cursing as he gets out to inspect the car. He continues to swear as he checks the tyre that went into a pothole.

Peter also gets out of the car and stands by it and gazes into the wood. A crow caws in the distance and he continues staring into the wood as if having a premonition.

'It looks okay.' Ryan reports as he walks back to the driver's side of the car.

Peter continues to stare at the wood – as if in a trance.

'Peter!' Ryan shouts out.

'Yes, yes sorry.' Peter replies as he opens the car door and slides back in.

'You okay?' Ryan turns the ignition.

'Yes, yes I'm fine.'

'Okay – let's not get spooky okay, driving through a wood to see a witch is spooky enough.'

Peter smiles back at him as the Chevrolet pulls out of the lay-by and accelerates up a hill churning up dried leaves and dust in its path.

They come to a small bridge which goes over a creek. Ryan applies the brakes to the car.

'Hmmm does this bridge look secure and safe to you?'

'You sure Contiana is not lurking in the wood nearby waiting for us to come to our demise so she can use us for spells or supper for that matter?' He continues in jest.

Peter laughs out loud 'Don't be silly, yes it should be safe – Contiana would have said otherwise.'

So Ryan puts the car into gear and slithers across the bridge. The weight of the bridge drops a little. 'I can almost see Contiana stirring her gigantic pot now smiling in anticipation.' He grips the steering wheel whilst moving as slowly as possible over the bridge.

'You are funny.' Peter nervously attempts to lighten the atmosphere.

Whilst the drop from the creek would not necessarily kill them, it would be a massive inconvenience. The car coasts along the bridge that spans approximately 200 yards. It slowly goes over a bump just at the end of the crossing.

'Gosh my poor car. If I knew it was going to be this bad I would have insisted we hired a car under your expense and insurance.'

Peter remains silent – he has learnt in situations like this it is best to stay quiet.

They make it over the bridge and they come to a fork in the road – by the side of the fork in the road ahead of them there is a murder of crows on the ground, they appear to be scavenging on something...something dead.

Ryan turns the steering wheel following Peter's pointing finger to take the left turn. Peter points whilst keeping his eyes on the meandering feathered blackness on the other side.

'Strange that they're not scared, and flying away with our approach huh?' Peter proclaims, glad that they are taking the turning away from the crows.

'Yes very strange.' Ryan replies.

As if choreographed the crows all rise at the same time – lifting like dense smog from an oil industry. The cawing is intense and the birds scatter in different directions. A carcass of a half eaten deer lies where the crows have just dispersed. Both Peter and Ryan wince.

'It's not long now, just down that path; we should see the house in a minute or so from what I remember. I only came here once with Jaime.' Peter estimates.

In about a minute or so an old cottage covered in ivy is revealed right in the middle of the wood. A big yellow rose bush is situated at the right side of the house. The cottage resembles an illustration he had seen of the house of candy in the children's fairy tale; Hansel and Gretel, except this building was not made of sweets.

'Here we are.' Peter exclaims. 'I remember it well now, still as quaint and characteristic as ever.'

A lady sashays out of the house on to a path. She is wearing a frilly white cotton dress and has wavy hair that has been dyed an electric blue. There is something fey and exuberant about her.

"I know you're a white witch but a frilly white dress – really?" Ryan thinks to himself.

'Hello, hello!' Contiana yells.

"As expected, eccentric as a bag of nuts and bolts." Ryan thinks to himself again.

'Hi.' Ryan utters with a smile, hoping it's sincere.

'Hello Contiana, how the devil are you?' Peter announces and smiles after realising what he's just said.

'You do remember I am a white witch right?' Contiana remarks smiling, she reaches out to give Peter a hug and whispers something in his ear.

Ryan reaches into the boot of his car to grab a bag and as he does so he turns round to ask a question. 'It will be okay to use a Dictaphone to record our chat right?'

'Certainly.' Contiana pulls away from the embrace with Peter.

'Let's go in I've made us some savoury biscuits to have with a nice cup of tea.' Contiana leads the way into her home.

Ryan and Peter follow and on reaching the doorway a strong smell of sandalwood and jasmine emanates from the house. A little porch leads into the living room, which is medium sized with a fireplace and a stone cobbled floor. A huge red patterned rug owns most of the floor and somehow compliments four different kinds of arm chairs and a bench. An old radio sits on a small table next to a chestnut wooden bookshelf to the right side of the living room. The bookshelf appears to be the only valuable furniture in the lounge. Lit candles are scattered all around. Following on through the lounge a small hallway leads into a kitchen.

'Please follow me, follow me.' Contiana beckons with pride as she continues to walk through the small hallway. Her white dress gracefully moves from side to side in rhythm to her steps.

A few pictures are scattered around the walls, some of them are holiday snapshots of her in Thailand. Amongst the array of pictures are also some quotes and all are encased in beautifully wacky frames, including one which simulate being covered in cobwebs.

"There's a cliché right there." Ryan thinks to himself.

The fragrance lessens a little now as they approach the kitchen which is considerably bigger than the lounge and appears more like the living room as it also has comfortable seating furniture which includes a sofa. Ryan smiles secretly as he is pleasantly relieved they are not going to be sitting in the lounge, he was concerned about the strong redolence of jasmine and sandalwood. The scent is bearable in the kitchen. He also wishes for Contiana's sake that the candles are not paraffin candles as that could not be doing her lungs any good.

A round table with chairs and cushions perfectly arranged is situated next to a traditional dark green agar. On the worktop - which is granite; various herbs, jars and coloured bottles of different shapes and sizes are arranged. Different candles flicker albeit not as many as in the lounge which would account for the milder fragrance. Ryan is sure that they are paraffin candles and wonders to himself if she realizes the harm paraffin can cause. On the stove a copper kettle whistles away and Contiana reaches for it and turns the cooker off.

'Please make yourself comfortable – you're both welcome to my humble abode.' She gets tea bags from chinaware that is highly decorated with paintings of ivy; it replicates the outside of her house. She places the tea bags in a large blue teapot and pours in hot water.

Ryan and Peter pull out a chair each and both sit down almost in unison.

'Both happy with tea?'

'That would be lovely.' Peters replies whilst Ryan nods.

Contiana pours the tea in simple non-fancy white mugs and she pulls out a chair and sits down. She reaches out both her hands and gestures for the guys to put out their hands and she takes hold of them.

'I ask for a circle of peace and harmony as we have our chat.' Contiana grins with a twinkle in her eye.

Ryan remembers a study on Ultrahaptics, a system that creates tactile sensations using ultrasound. People can recognise different emotional states from tactile clues on their hands. He wonders if Contiana is innately aware of this phenomenon.

'Oh, oh almost forgot.' Contiana rises from her chair and goes out to the back door which leads into an exotically proud garden. It is pristine and full of colours from different plants. She bends down over a sizeable plant pot situated by the back door and digs out five large crystals of varying colours and shapes. She cleans them as she comes back into the kitchen. Ryan steals a quick glance at Peter which Contiana notices. She blows at the crystals in her hands, dispelling more of the soil and she places them on the table and then picks up one of the lit candles from the work top and sits back down at the table.

'Now.' She gasps, 'let's begin.....Oh Ryan.' She turns to Ryan. 'Burying the crystals in the soil overnight replenishes their crystallic power so to speak.'

'I see.' Ryan simply replies whilst stealing another more subdued glance at Peter. Peter pulls out a picture of his partner which he had in his book and places it on the table by the candle. Ryan glances at Peter again and portrays one of those smiles that although forced is meant to be endearing. He places his Dictaphone in the centre of the table.

Peter returns a somewhat awkward smile at Ryan. "Could Contiana be right, does he really fancy me?" He thinks to himself.

'The last time that I saw Jaime was about six months ago – as you know he was carrying out research here in

Clophill about witchcraft which is where I come in and I remember him being very passionate about the research. Indeed he wanted a true account of modern witchcraft whilst taking on the history and entwining it with the present.'

'Was there anything that made you think he might have been in danger at all?' Peter asks whilst scratching his left arm.

'Nooo…however he did say that he felt something weird at the cemetery, he was convinced that someone was watching him although he didn't feel threatened by this.' Contiana clarifies as she pours tea in each of the mugs.

'Did he say how often he had this feeling and would you happen to know the exact day that he had this feeling?' Ryan asked.

'I don't actually remember the exact day but I do believe he told me about three occurrences where he was convinced someone was watching him from a hedge near the church at the cemetery. He did say once that he called out, I think that was the day before he disappeared. He said he could have sworn he heard a shuffle in the hedge and then nothing.'

'Did he say anymore on why he did not feel threatened?' Peter asks whilst folding his arms and placing them on the table.

'Not really – I think over all he felt safe in the village as everyone was so nice to him, plus he only ever went to the cemetery in the day time. I guess if he visited at night it might have been a different story.'

'Which day did he visit you last, can you remember?' Ryan takes a sip of his tea.

'Again I'm afraid I'm not sure of the exact day.' Contiana confesses apologetically.

Suddenly Peter sits up in his chair. 'Do you know which bed and breakfast Jaime stayed in whilst carrying out his research?'

'I believe it was the Dragons Inn, although I'm not sure which one. Two of them exist in the village you see.'

'Yea why is that? Why are there two of the same named pubs in such a small village?' Ryan interrogates.

'Well...How do I explain this?' Contiana scratches her head and parts a wavy lock of hair.

She observes both men and whilst touching her crystals she conveys.

'A strong superstition runs deep in Clophill. Has to be two of every significant communal building. The locals strongly believe there is a parallel universe alongside our universe and only having one named entity or place or building is bad luck.'

'Come again.' Ryan checks both what he's heard and the Dictaphone.

'People here believe there is another dimension to Clophill, putting it plainly.' Contiana continues.

Peter leans in. 'Was Jaime aware of this?'

'Yes he was, in fact he stirred his story towards that in the end, started doing research on quantum physics.' Contiana discloses whilst reaching for her cup of tea.

'Quantum Physics?' Ryan remains baffled.

'Yes - a lot of research is being done in Quantum physics that is opening up new possibilities, well not even possibilities – truths, that our reality is not as it seems – the only reality we know is the one we perceive but our sensory perception is limited. Quantum physics is finally bringing science and relig….. well, spirituality together.' Contiana continues.

'Well, I never…..fascinating, did not expect this at all. Getting a science lecture from a witch, and oh I'm saying that with the greatest respect by the way.' Ryan adds whilst checking the Dictaphone is still recording.

'That's okay, I'm not easily offended.' Contiana reassures, smiling.

'Did Jaime leave any notes, clues as to where he could have been meeting with anyone else other than you?' Peter clasps his hands on the table.

'There was another person. He said he found him fascinating to listen to.' Contiana answers.

Ryan quickly takes a glance at Peter.

'Did he say what they talked about?' Peter pretends not to be bothered by what Contiana has said or indeed the quick glance Ryan had given him.

'I think the guy knew quite a lot about quantum physics and recent discoveries on the subject.' Contiana continues.

'I don't suppose you happen to know this guy's name or where to get hold of him?' Ryan enquires.

'I'm not sure the guy was from around here – I think he too was visiting.'

Ryan takes another concealed glance at Peter.

'Lloyd….I think his name was Lloyd. They both came here once to see me.'

'Oh.' Peter remarks leaning in on the table. 'So you met him?'

'Yes he seemed like a nice enough fellow. He was balding, had narrow eyes that were quite close together. He certainly fit the profile of an independent confident fellow, with great attention to detail.'

'What do you mean?' Ryan asks.

'Oh, people with close set eyes tend to be detail oriented and independent.' Contiana explains.

'I see.' Ryan says.

'Any idea where this guy Lloyd was staying?' Peter moves back to centre position in his chair.

'I believe he was also staying at the Dragons Inn. That's how they met.' Contiana mentions innocently.

This time Ryan keeps his eyes on the table.

'Well that's good; we should be able to find out from the Inn by asking people. They might well know his whereabouts. For all we know he might still be in the village.' Peter suppresses the slight anxiety and insecurity he is beginning to feel.

'I must say Peter that you are close to him. He is around you somehow. It's a very strong bond. The bond between you and Jaime – He loves you dearly and often talked about you when he visited. You will find him.' Contiana reassures with quiet conviction.

'Thank you Contiana….thank you so much.' Peter acknowledges whilst taking a deep breath. 'I hope so. I really do.'

Ryan considers Peter and smiles whilst taking in a deep breath too.

'I believe we have taken up enough of your time.' Peter says whilst getting up, placing his hands on his pockets and consciously checking as usual.

'You're both very welcome anytime.' Contiana gets up.

'Not sure I said it but you have a lovely place here.' Ryan expresses just before turning the Dictaphone off.

'Thank you. Like I said, both welcome back anytime…...The cemetery; I suggest you both go there. There are clues.' Contiana prophesies.

'Okay.' Ryan and Peter say almost in unison. 'Thanks again.'

All three walk towards the door and Contiana reaches for Peter's arm pulling him towards her and gives him a hug and whispers something in his ear again.

Both men walk back to the car and Peter enters. Ryan stops by the car and turns around to Contiana. 'That Bridge….is it safe?'

'The old bridge you came over – yes it's safe. I can see why you may be concerned. It does look decrepit, but it's been built by crafted men who took pride in their work. They don't have builders like the old days.' She declares and turns to go back into her house.

Ryan turns to open the car door and as he does so a creaking sound originates from the bough of a tree close by, he looks in that direction and notices the tree writhing in the wind and each time it does so it creaks. He suddenly remembers a scene in the movie 'The Evil Dead' and he hurriedly gets in his car and starts the ignition.

Chapter 8

A fox scuttles through shrubbery and comes out into an open field. It gazes ahead nervously and then sneaks across the field to the next shelter. It scurries past an old cabin. The cabin is small but looks in good condition. A flower pot containing a cannabis plant is outside by the door. Next to the pot is a wind chime which is making sweet music in rhythm to a slight breeze. Inside the cabin a man is waking up. He stretches and swings his legs over to the floor and gets up with a bounce. He is wearing boxer shorts, which reveal strong legs. He is tall with a good physique. He walks over to the kitchenette and puts on a coffee making machine. On the table close by is a book entitled "What the bleep do we know." He reaches for it and flips through the pages whilst anticipating his morning and coffee.

A beeping noise makes the man drop the book and reach for his phone which is wedged in armchair close to him.

'Hello, Lloyd speaking.'

He listens intently and then. 'Hello I can't hear you please speak up.'

He holds the phone away from him staring at it as if by some hypnotic miracle he will make the phone work.

'Stupid mobile phones – what's the point.' He mutters to himself and throws the phone back on the armchair and goes over to salvage his coffee from the beeping coffee machine. The hi-tech machine is out of place in the sparsely furnished old fashioned cottage.

He sits down whilst grabbing the book and takes a sip of his coffee. He stretches out in the armchair and places the book down between his legs and ponders. He reaches for the cup of coffee and takes another sip. A creak makes him turn instantly towards the door.

Lloyd is a black man 5 foot and 10 inches tall with short hair on the sides and a balding top. It compliments a finely sculpted beard. He has dark brown eyes a big nose and thick lips that accentuate a primal attractiveness which most sexual beings would find irresistible.

Lloyd has Asperger's Syndrome and was an only child to his parents who gave him up for adoption. His adoptive parents gave him all the support and care he needed to counteract his social inadequacies and he had a fantastic education with a private tutor. This nonetheless did not stop him from craving and being obsessed with less than normal interests.

He loves quantum physics and always wanted to be a professor in the subject. He had only one sexual interest but alas it did not work out and so he never tried again he seemed akin to be attracted to other men who weren't emotionally available.

His biggest fear was being alone even though he mastered being on his own and his whole psyche and lack of social prowess guide him towards being on his own.
It was a dilemma. A paradox onto himself.

Meanwhile Peter and Ryan pull up outside a cemetery; a derelict church reluctantly stands nearby, with odd graffiti on the walls. Both men get out of the car almost on cue.

'So what did Contiana whisper to you when we left?'

'She told me not to worry, that Lloyd and Jaime did not get it on.'

'Really, she said that?'

'Yes.' Peter simply says.

'And when we arrived at the place, what did she whisper to you then?' Ryan interrogates further, this time avoiding a broken branch on the ground.

'You don't miss a thing do you?'

'Well, I am a detective.'

'She just whispered welcome.' Peter lies and hates that he does so, he has never liked lying, not even white lies to protect the feelings of people.

They approach an open cemetery with lots of yew trees.

'Lovely sombre place to reflect on.' Peter smiles in an attempt to soften the mood and change the subject.

A few yards away on a tombstone, a black bird stares at the men cautiously.

'Well there's a cliché.' Ryan retorts with an uncomfortable smile.

'A raven.' Peter alleges whilst wondering if Contiana was right about Ryan fancying him. He was never great at knowing and his "gaydar" was rubbish.

'How do you know it's not a crow?'

At that precise moment the bird makes a guttural gronk gronk noise.

'Because of that sound.' Peter adds. 'Besides, crows often fly in groups – A raven will often be on its own, they're more cautious and less social. Their feathers are also a lot shinier than a Crow's.'

Both men move towards the tombstone, which is unusually large and seems out of place in the cemetery.

They are both drawn towards this particular tombstone. The Raven continues to stare at them as they approach.

'More cautious you say?' Ryan looks at Peter.

'Yea...supposed to be.'

The Raven retains its focus, resembling a statue, as if part of the tombstone.

'Did you know that they also live to about 22 years longer that a Crow?' Peter boasts in an attempt to distract from the anxiety starting to conjure up in his being.

'I honestly don't care about that right now – why is that damn bird not moving?'

'I really don't...' The Raven suddenly flies off but not before appearing to bow its head.

'Did it just bow its head at us?'

'Don't be silly.' Peter utters.

They both continue towards the tombstone, their hands raised up slightly so as to avoid getting scratched by bramble. They both rely on their jeans in not getting scratched, as they saunter through shrub.

On reaching the tombstone, which is chalky stone and has weathered a little. The men observe the etchings.

JOANNE FABER

18 – 197

The rest of the numbers have weathered away.

Peter bends down to clear some dead leaves at the base and finds some kind of marking. He examines the side of the tombstone and drops into a sitting position - a startled expression on his face.

'What's the matter?' Ryan asks.

On the side of the Tombstone is a symbol ♏.

Lloyd strides towards the door which is ajar but not before spilling some of his coffee down his trousers. He curses as he wipes his leg. He can now hear a faint tapping. He walks right up to the door and pushes the door open.

A Raven flies up to a banister and perches on a rail and stares at Lloyd.

'Shoooo!' Lloyd shouts. The bird flies off and disappears into the wood.

'Strange.' He mutters to himself.

He turns to walk back in. He strolls over to get what remains of his coffee and he downs it in one swig.

The phone rings again and this time he hurriedly grabs the phone and rushes outside to answer it.

'Hello, Lloyd speaking.' He exhales with relief.

'Yes, I can hear you – Is everything okay?'

He listens intently. 'Okay that's fine, please do let me know the outcome as soon as possible.' He never did like saying ASAP; he felt it was overly bossy and unnecessarily serious. Even in emails he chose to write it out in full – he found it more jovial whilst still stating urgency.

'I am still in the cottage yes – should be here for a couple more days.'

Pause.

'Uh huh.' Lloyd pulls on a wood splinter on one of the panels to the front porch of the cottage.

'Okay that's fine but what about Contiana?'

Pause.

'Uh huh...yup...okay.'

Pause.

'Okay that's fine, talk later, goodbye for now.'

Lloyd hangs up the phone and goes back for another coffee.

'I had a dream about this symbol.' Peter mutters still staring at the tombstone.

Ryan scans the tombstone then returns his attention to Peter.

Both men do not speak for a few seconds, the cawing of a crow resounds in the distance.

'Can you remember the dream – the whole dream?'

'Sort of, I was in a cemetery – and there were a lot of tombstones of children, I remember that.'

'Anything else?'

'There was a dead baby, a crying dead baby.' Peter peeks up at Ryan.

Ryan studies the tombstone. 'When you say a crying dead baby, what exactly do you mean?'

'It was dead; it had maggots falling out of its eye sockets.'

'Ok, that dead….. this sign.' Ryan points to the strange symbol ♉. 'Do you have any idea what it means?'

'No idea whatsoever.'

'It looks like some kind of ancient symbol.' Ryan mutters whilst bending down to move away some cock's foot grass.

'In the dream there were also the letters B, A and C.'

'A B C, the start of something perhaps?' Ryan suggests as he turns to Peter.

'The symbol could be a letter in some ancient alphabet.' Peter also suggests.

'Who do you think Joanne Faber is?'

'No idea but I'm going to find out, if it kills me.' With that Peter gets up off the ground and brushes his behind and legs with his hands.

'We need to get back, it's getting dark.' Peter says still brushing dead leaves from behind his legs.

'So.' Ryan says puzzled.

'So even though Jaime was not threatened at the cemetery, he only ever came here in daylight.'

'Oh.' Ryan utters.

'I wonder where their local library is?' Peter adds while feeling his pockets.

'I'm sure there's one in town.' Ryan claims as he pulls out his phone to Google - Library Clophill.

'Do you think that's why Contiana said to come here?' Peter is satisfied with the contents of his pockets.

'I presume so…it's strange that you see something on a gravestone that you dreamt about.'

'It is indeed.'

Peter and Ryan saunter back to the car, brushing past overgrown cow parsley and giant daisies as they do. They reach the border of the cemetery where there is a lot of blackthorn and cotoneaster in the hedge.

'That's weird.' Peter mumbles, observing the hedge.

'What is?' Ryan pushes one last tuft of cow parsley to the side.

'The hedge, there isn't any fruit. There should be fruit this time of year.'

'Never knew you were a botanist.' Ryan remarks exhaling a little as he finally gets clear of the last cow parsley.

Peter walks up to the hedge and inspects further. 'No fruit and no buds.'

'It's probably just a stressed plant or the seasons are messed up a little- let's face it, with climate change the seasons are all over the place recently.'

'Never knew you were a climatologist.' Peter jests.

'Tooshay.' Ryan replies.

'C'mon let's get out of here.' Peter asserts whilst walking in the direction of their parked car.

Lloyd sits in an armchair with an acquired taste in upholstery. He's reading a book entitled 'Ampersand &', he peers over his spectacles and gazes at the opened door to the cottage. He stares outside for a while even though nothing noticeable grabs his attention, he is deep in thought, eventually he returns to his book. He turns a page and then peers over his glasses again; it's as if he's expecting something to show up. Nothing does.

Peter and Ryan pull up outside the Dragon's Inn and Peter exits the car.

'Thanks for driving Ryan.'

'You're welcome, tomorrow I'll do some enquiries and you check some stuff out in the library tomorrow about symbolic writing and the name Joanne Faber.'

'Yep will do.' Peter responds as he shuts the car door.

'Oh also see if you can find out anything to do with the superstition in the town over the parallel universe whilst you're at it. Shedding some light on that should be interesting. I will ask some questions too my end.'

'Okay, will do.' Peter replies.

Chapter 9

Peter and Jaime sit on a plum coloured blanket having a picnic in a glade surrounded by ancient woodland. A radio DJ is interviewing a professor in Quantum Physics. The broadcast emanates from a snazzy digital radio lying on its side on the blanket. Jaime has his head in Peter's lap and Peter delicately drops a cherry tomato into Jaime's mouth.

'Mmm can I have the next one glazed in the pomegranate sauce please?' Jaime winces as he bites into the tomato.

'You can have something else glazed in pomegranate sauce if you like.' Peter jests whilst reaching for Jaime's crotch and gently squeezing it.

'You're so saucy.' Jaime stretches his head upwards for a kiss. As they both smooch they laugh into each other's mouths as they realise the pun.

Jaime pulls back and gazes deep into Peter's eyes.

'I do too.' Peter whispers and they both kiss again.

'You know I had given up when we met at the library.'

'Given up?'

'Given up on dating.' Jaime snuggles into Peter's lap.

'I had too; I found the dating game excruciating.'

'I know...it's as if it was a ritual from a whole different universe – I just didn't get it.'

'Having to watch that you didn't offend because of our bluntness with the truth.'

'I guess you have to be super comfortable with someone in order to share the truth all the time.'

'So glad I found you.' Peter proclaims whilst stroking Jaime's head.

They remain in silence for a while, breathing in the present moment.

'Remember when in the past I would have said something silly to break up the mood cause I felt awkward.' Jaime smiles, whilst enjoying having his head pampered.

'I do, it's funny how easily afraid or uncomfortable we become when expressing our true selves. We want to avoid the present by any means.' Peter takes a deep breath as he continues to stroke Jaime's head.

'Not anymore, I want you to continue to pull me up when I'm trying to get out of the present moment Peter. I appreciate it.'

Both men admire each other deeply and Jaime lifts himself up off of Peter's lap.

'Did you feel that?'

'Yes I think I did.' Peter agrees scanning the glade.

'That has to be the strongest déjà vu I've ever felt.' In that precise moment cackling interference interrupts the Professor's voice for a few moments before fine tuning again.

'Now that was eerie.' Peter pulls on his lower lip.

'Very eerie.' Jaime replies.

Peter wakes up, sits up in bed and scans his surroundings. He can't remember where he is. He tries to make sense of what he is witnessing. The silhouette of someone is staring at him from a window, he is about to have palpitations then realises he's staring at his reflection in the mirror across the room in the Dragon's Inn.

He gets up and checks his phone for the time and it's just gone past 3am.

He's always had issues with sleep, especially since Jaime disappeared from his life.

Peter wonders if what he had was a dream or a memory. Jaime and he had spent a lot of romantic times in that glade and some of their most cherished moments were experienced there.

He rises, grabs a cup and fills it with water from a jug, drinks it and then fills it up again and returns to bed. He is drowsy and hopes that when he tucks in and tries to focus on his breathing he falls back to sleep. He is very familiar now with those times when it will be near impossible to fall back into slumber, but tonight was not one of them. His mind was not racing as much, so he had a chance.

Peter turns over, embracing a memory of spooning Jaime and he shuts his eyes and breathes slowly and deeply. Before long he is back in the glade.

Ryan is standing in his hotel room and he is talking on the phone. His hotel room is decorated in warm colours and has furniture almost identical to Peter's room.

'I know that I promised and I am going to make it up to her, I am – I just feel the need to help this guy out. Please understand. You know that I will make it up to her.'

'I know you will - it's not as if this is normal, I'll put her on the phone and you tell her, okay?'

'Thanks Teresa, I really appreciate it.'

A little girl answers the phone. 'Dad?'

'Hello my gorgeous.' Ryan announces with a smile.

'I am so sorry I have to cancel our meeting but I promise I will make it up to you okay.'

'Okay daddy, are you working?'

'I am...I'm trying to help someone find their partner, someone he loves very much.'

'Is he gay daddy, like you?'

'He is my precious, he is.'

'I hope he finds him daddy, you help him okay.'

'I will Chloe, I will – how did you get so smart?'

'Because you and mummy are smart.' Chloe simply replies.

'That is right my gorgeous girl, that is right.' Ryan says as he sheds a tear.

'I know somewhere, some other place you and mummy and me are together.' Chloe says in a quieter tone.

'What do you mean baby girl?' Ryan straightens up and focuses as if to catch every word that comes out of his daughter's mouth with great care.

'Somewhere else, in another place you're not gay daddy, and you're with mummy and that makes me very happy.'

Ryan puts the phone down by his chest and is unable to control the tears streaming down his face. He attempts to swallow the sadness filled up in his throat before responding to his daughter.

'I am with you baby girl, I always will be, okay, always, I'm your dad…...nothing changes that.'

'I know daddy, I know.'

'Let me speak to mum again – I will see you next week okay. You be good for mummy okay. Love you.'

'I will daddy, love you too.'

Teresa comes back on the line. 'Are you okay?'

'Yes I'm fine, just a little thrown by what she said that's all.'

'She's a smart girl, and you have an amazing relationship with her.'

'Thanks for saying that, you're a fantastic mum, she's very lucky.'

'You look after yourself okay.'

'I will, thanks again Teresa.........for being you.'

'Bye for now.' The phone goes dead and Ryan stands and holds the phone to his ear as if cherishing the moment.

Ryan is a 39 year old man who married very early in his teens. Only a year ago he came out as gay. He remained good friends with Teresa even though it was heartbreaking for her finding out that her husband was gay. She held onto the fact that they created a beautiful girl together and that would always be precious.

Ryan had always struggled with the gay life not really fitting in but he was still grateful for coming out of the closet. It was a great risk, coming out, as he truly loved Teresa and did not want to hurt her but since being himself he knew that he was being an authentic and better dad to their little girl.

He had always been interested in detective work since he was eight years old. He was obsessed with Agatha Christie books and read them every chance he got. His father was abusive to his mum and had finally left them only to be found dead in a river a few months later. He had fallen over a bridge in a drunken stupor. Ryan always thought this was a great relief as they could get on with their lives in peace. Ryan was the only son and he loved his mum immensely, which is why it was earth shattering when his mum died to cancer a few years back. He was always grateful that he at least got to tell his mum about his sexuality. He had sought counselling to help him with his grief and in the process had realised that there was unresolved resentment for his dad. Teresa was a massive help to him and had brought passion into his life after so many years of merely existing. He would always be eternally grateful for this and would cherish and do anything for Teresa and he was pleased that Teresa knew that.

Ryan admires anyone with a power of reasoning and believes strongly that intelligence and reasoning does not necessarily correlate.

A rotund man sits in an armchair smoking a cigarette, up above him are various framed certificates. One of them reads '*In commemoration of your service to the Parish.*' He swings his chair round and then struggles up reaching for the phone on his mahogany desk.

The room is likened to a small lounge more so than an office. The walls are painted dark green except the wall where his desk backs into which is a shade of light red.

Sunlight filters through venetian blinds that are half closed on a large window behind his desk.

'Yes hello it's Donald; please can you patch me through to Nicholas.'

After a few seconds Donald sits back down in his chair and extinguishes the cigarette.

'Hello, yes you do remember you were supposed to call me right?'

'Uh huh, well it's 5 minutes past so...Never mind apologising, just ensure that you stick to the time agreed next time or I will get someone to replace you. Now where were we on the community funding project?'

A faint knock on the door makes Donald shout with a guttural voice. 'Come in!' and he coughs down the phone.

'Yes carry on.' He bellows, as he clears his throat further.

A man in a suit enters and appears docile. Donald signals to him to come in.

'Yes, that's fine you do that.' He slams the phone down.

'Yes Victor, what's up?'

'It's the issue with the press regarding the car accident – there is a reporter that doesn't want to let it lie I'm afraid.'

'Then perhaps we should make him lie...down, permanently.'

Victor fidgets on the spot and picks at his fingers.

'Relax, joke, God, can't get any fun around here.'

Victor forces a smile.

'Arrange a meeting with him and ...'

'He's a she.'

'Oh, well arrange a meeting with her – this should be interesting.'

'Your calendar has a clear slot next week.'

'Then arrange the meeting for then Victor, thank you.' And with that he waves his hand for him to leave as he reaches for the phone again. He also opens a drawer by his side and gets out a contraption that looks like a bullet. He puts it to his nose and snorts and then places it back in the drawer.

'Yes Donald here, do I have to be concerned about the reporter fishing over the car accident a few days ago? Uh huh, okay well keep me informed – use my private number.'

There is a knock on the door again.

'Come in!'

Victor enters sheepishly. 'Do you want the plumbers round to investigate the smell tomorrow? They have a free slot.'

'What sme...Oh yea, the supposed smell coming from the sewers which I cannot smell myself. Yes, yes tell them to do what they need to do. Anything to stop you guys fucking going on about it.'

With that Victor backs out of the office and closes the door.

Donald was an only child and it was a good thing as his parents were incapable of bringing him up. They were callous, detached and unloving. Their idea of parenting was lavishing with gifts and presents and that was pretty much it. Donald learnt to get what he wanted when he wanted regardless of what he had to do to get it. Because when he screamed in the shop for something long enough his mum always gave in and got it him. His parents later divorced because of his dad's gambling addiction and his mum attempted to bring him up on her own dividing the attention between the men that came to have sex with her in their home.

Donald learnt to switch off his emotions and was devoid of any conscience. When he was 12 years old he particularly took delight in killing bugs and placing different species in a glass bottle so that they fought each other.

One thing he did which he never told anyone was empty a lot of biting ants from a glass jar into a pram with a toddler and then run off down the road. But this was not as shameful as fucking his neighbour's dog in a hedge when he turned 16. He always consoled himself with the fact that at least the dog was a bitch. He mostly never gave any of these incidents any significance or attention. Albeit a morsel of conscience or shame lingered somewhere preventing him from sharing these episodes of his life with anyone. He visited the bookies every chance he got to take his mind off things. He placed bets on horses and dogs with no discrimination which was ironic as he went through life discriminating.

Donald opens the drawer again, retrieves and sniffs at his bullet.

Chapter 10

Peter conveniently spots the library sign as he walks out of the Inn. He marches in that direction. A big sun is rising, pouring crisp golden light all over the village. Mornings like these Peter always described as having magic in the air. It made him feel anything was possible. All the environmental factors had to be just right, the light, humidity and temperature. It could only ever be in the mornings as the light was softer and it was before the raucousness of human existence dominated. What refined these magical mornings was if it had just rained. But this morning it hadn't and it didn't matter. Bird song and the rustling of leaves on tree branches resound. Mornings like these did not happen often and it was hard to ascertain whether the feeling induced was a culmination of inner feelings from the day before and or state of mind at the time. Nonetheless, moments like these should not be rationalised only enjoyed mindfully and he intended to do just that.

He follows the sign for the direction of the library, the last sign said 2.5 miles. He thinks about Jaime, try as he might to stop thinking about him and remain present to the moment, he struggles; he misses him so much it's hard to be in the now. He attempts to throw him out of his mind whilst taking a deep breath. He pays attention to his surroundings. A Volkswagen slowly goes past with a number plate that reads B3N DER. He wonders whether this is deliberate. He discreetly peers into the vehicle to scan the driver and from what he can see; nothing about him looks gay at all. Then the driver turns to Peter and he spots his eyebrows. They are trimmed.

Peter smiles as he continues to walk along the path. He smiles even more when a lorry drives past with the word GAYWOOD printed across the side. "What are the chances?"

He disturbs a crow attacking a bin bag on the side of the road. The black bird punctures a hole in the bag, fishing for something with its beak. It's startled and flies away and perches on a fence. Peter imagines the crow's disdain at him for interrupting his breakfast. It caws loudly and Peter is forced to remember the crow that was on the tombstone in the cemetery. Then he remembers the murder of crows that were by the side of the road.

A little girl strides towards him and Peter checks to see if any responsible adults are accompanying her and he can't find anyone. He glances at the young girl; she can't be more than 6 years old. She looks down at her feet as she continues to walk towards him. A stupendous highway maintenance truck whirls clumsily around the corner on the road ahead of them. It produces a cacophony of excruciating noises as it goes over speed bumps in the road. Metal objects in the back of the truck clunk loudly on each bump and violent painful gear changes reverberate as the driver attempts to manoeuvre the truck and slow down.

The little girl is almost up to him on the walkway. The truck driver has slowed right down; he goes over one last bump in the road. There is a loud clanking of metal again as something in the back of the truck is flung around. The din causes anxiety in Peter; he has never liked loud noises, certainly not sudden loud noises. He remembers a time when he could not even pull the cork out of a bottle of bubbly for fear of the popping noise it would make.

The little girl now passes him and she is wearing an old fashioned lilac dress as if she had walked out of a film set for a period drama. Peter turns around as she strides past and at that precise moment she glimpses up at him and mutters:

'There are other b...'

A deafening clanking noise instantly fills the air, followed by a screeching sound of the truck's brakes as it halts at a pedestrian crossing. The cacophony startles and jitters Peter's already frazzled nerves and he stares at the truck driver with disdain. He hurriedly returns his attention to where the little girl was and she is nowhere to be seen.

Ryan is sitting outside a cafe having coffee and reading a newspaper. The cafe is simple, nothing fancy. Ryan has chosen this particular cafe as in the distance he can see the old church which is part of the cemetery Peter and him visited the day before. Four people sit around him; one couple chatting on one table and a toddler with an older person who could be an older sister or his mum on another table. A waiter comes outside and attends to the couple asking them if they would like more coffee. Both of them politely decline.

The waiter turns towards the adult and the kid and nods his head and the adult puts her hand up and turns her attention back to the kid. The waiter then turns to Ryan and rushes towards him causing Ryan to be startled slightly; he is saved by his mobile phone ringing and he reaches for it as the waiter approaches his table. Ryan puts his hand up as he answers the phone. The waiter turns around and trots back indoors.

'Hello.' Ryan answers the phone with slight relief.

Pause.

'I see, and just the name Faber on its own?'

Ryan observes the waiter as he listens to the person on the phone; the waiter is watching him which makes him uncomfortable. Ryan decides to turn around in his chair and continues to listen to his caller.

'And anything on Contiana?'

Ryan takes a peek at the waiter who is now serving someone inside the cafe.

'Sorry did you say Lloyd?'

'STOP IT!' The adult shouts at the kid on the table next to Ryan. Ryan's heart increases its tempo and he tries to control his breathing. He wonders why he is so jumpy, he is never this nervous.

'Okay, please let me know of anything else you find.' With that Ryan hangs up the phone.

He returns to his paper and spots an article about an autopsy to be carried out on the recent casualty in a freak car accident. He checks the name of the author and it's a woman called Caroline Fletcher.

Chapter 11

Donald sits at his desk, fingering something with a smile; he's tormenting a daddy long-leg. Both wings are lying by the side of the little creature and he very carefully pulls at its hind leg until it comes off. Old habits die hard. The creature attempts to pull away with its front legs and Donald holds it back with his finger pressing down on the other hind leg. A knock on the door startles Donald who swiftly brushes the insect off his desk.

'Come in!' He shouts wiping the smile off his face.

Victor enters. 'Miss Fletcher is here sir.'

'Good, show her in.'

Victor walks back out and after a moment a lady with a strong posture walks into the office. She is wearing a suit and has short auburn hair. She has little makeup on and for a lady has a somewhat prominent jaw line. She struts straight up to Donald and shakes his hand while introducing herself.

'Thanks for taking the time to see me.'

'Don't thank me yet – you may not be getting the outcome you planned for.' Donald remains seated.

'Quite okay – I never have expectations; I certainly don't have attachments to possible outcomes.' Caroline reaches for a chair and sits down. 'I find that keeps me flexibly adaptive.' Caroline adds with a smile on her face.

Donald stares at Caroline for a moment and then reaches for his drawer and removes a couple of cough lozenges. He offers Caroline one just using a face gesture.

'No thanks, I'm good.'

'Okay why don't we get straight down to business?' Donald asserts as he returns one lozenge to the drawer, closes it and unwraps the other.

'That would be a wise use of our time.' Caroline comments with an even broader smile.

Donald sucks on his sweet, rolling it around in his mouth noisily as he does so. He gawps at Caroline somewhat sternly, scanning her presence with predatory eyes.

'Where would you like to start?' Caroline retrieves her Dictaphone out of what looks like a cross between a satchel and a handbag.

'I'm assuming you have no objection to me using this.' She gestures with her face at the Dictaphone.

'No, that's fine – I got nothing to hide.'

Caroline was an only child and she was very close to her parents who brought her up the best they could. It was devastating for both her and her father when her mum passed away to ovarian cancer. Her dad had recently been admitted into a care home for people with dementia and she visited him every chance she got.

She had had setbacks like most people in life. Someone had attempted to rape her down a cul-de sac one late festive evening when returning from a friend's house party. She was quite tipsy. The guy had almost started to penetrate her when a passer-by frightened him off. The experience affected her drastically and she became housebound for a while, frightened of her own shadow. She embarked on an anxiety eradication program and a combat training course and after about a year she built back her self confidence and promised herself never to be intimidated by a man ever again.

She changed careers from being a project manager to being a reporter as she wanted a new challenge and some excitement in her life after splitting up with her partner.

'I'm just going to dive straight in Donald...Can I call you Donald?'

'Yea that's fine, Donald is my name.' Donald sits up in his chair and repositions himself, as if preparing for battle.

'The accident on the A233 is still somewhat of a mystery, to me at least, and I wondered why the insistence on closing the case?'

'It was a freak accident – the poor guy had an aneurysm and crashed his car into a tree. What more is there to investigate?'

'The guy was dehydrated almost beyond recognition. There is no reason why he would have been that way. It doesn't make sense.'

'The guy had no one who could identify him, no family member or friend.' Donald bellows.

'Well, exactly, don't you find that somewhat strange?'

'Well, the police have closed the case and they are the ones that investigate cases, not reporters.' Donald subconsciously places his hand over a Universal Serial Bus (USB) stick next to a green folder on his desk.

'Well, I suspect there's something more to it and I will continue to ask questions – it's my duty as a reporter to seek the truth.'

'Is it now?' Donald sucks his hard boiled sweet with some vehemence.

'Of course you are free to do what you want, but you won't be getting any cooperation from me and I don't want you wasting police time either.' Donald moves the USB stick slightly to the side.

'Okay that's fine, but can I ask one more question?'

'Yes.' Donald finishes off his lozenge.

'Why are you so interested in this accident?'

'What do you mean?' Donald puts his hand over the USB stick again.

'Well, why are you so keen to have the case closed?'

'How do you figure that one out? The police investigated and confirmed it was a freak accident.'

'But you intervened, you were present at the scene and insisted that the case be sorted and closed as soon as possible, why?' Caroline sits up in her chair.

'Because any kind of accident plays on the mind of people in the community if not resolved quickly – it's always better to resolve as soon as possible.'

'With all...I don't buy that I'm afrai...'

'I don't really care if you buy it or not Caroline, now I have given you substantial amount of my time. I suggest you move on from this but if you want to keep at it, that's your perogati...'

'An officer I spoke to informed me that you showed unusual interest in the case.'

'And who will that officer be?'

'Afraid I can't tell you that.'

'Then I'm afraid I can't help, now if you don't mind I really must get on.' Donald gets up from his chair and trudges around his desk up to her and sneers.

Caroline rises and saunters to the door without saying a word. Donald stands and stares, squeezing his lips together in contempt as she leaves the office.

Chapter 12

A sombre lit police department quietens down after an unusually busy day in a small town. Hard rain battering the roof and window pane is the only dominant noise. From the outside the police station is a characteristically quaint listed building and has a blue lamp outside, marked police.

Inside, over in a corner of the open planned office are three officers who appear to be arguing. Above them is a close up poster of a cow's face with the caption *"Observe the now."* Large teary bovine eyes stare at the three men below.

'That was not the case at all...excuse the pun.' A middle aged police man stands up from his desk and searches for something on a stand-alone computer situated on a standing desk.

'There was strange humming which three people verified in the same vicinity of that accident.' The police man moves back so that the three officers can see his entries on the witness catalogue system displayed on the computer screen.

'John if that's the cas... truth then...What is it with us, we need to eradicate the word "case" from our vocabulary when we are discussing incidents.'

Everyone laughs. Peter has always been good at de-escalating heated up situations and especially uses this skill in the office to ensure harmony.

Peter grew up in a good family based on great values and the belief that everyone has an ability to shine in whatever it is that takes their passion. His parents were hippies and so were liberal in bringing both him and his brother up. He came out to his older brother when he was just fourteen. They were both very close and his brother supported him the whole way. His brother encouraged him to tell their parents about his sexuality and Peter did and as his brother said, it was all okay. Both parents embraced him and made attempts to include gay things in conversation as they were privy to the heterosexual world they lived in and how it must impact on Peter.

Peter's father was a sergeant in the police force and he was a much respected man and ever since Peter was 10 he dreamed of joining the police like his father. He did actually dream of being an FBI agent and was obsessed with the X files series. Having a crush on Mulder and even more so when he surfed the net and learnt he was hung. But the police force was the next best thing. Let's face it; he was never going to meet Fox Mulder.

Life was pretty good except for the cancer scare his mum had but that was all sorted with chemo and a healthy positive attitude and everything was back to normal in no time.

John stops laughing. 'Peter if that's true then I agree, we need to investigate further but three witness accounts aren't really sufficient to follow this up, it's a big area.'

'Yes a big area of a scarcely populated town.' Peter announces logging off from the computer.

'Okay, okay Peter I will come with you tonight. I will do that with you because you're my buddy. I'll try to remain open minded.'

'Thank you John.'

The other police man standing next to them gets up and claps his hands. 'So that's that then. Case solved.'

All three men laugh again and Peter and John walk one way and the other police man walks the other.

'So run your theory by me again– The humming causes the aneurysm somehow, a high pitched hum that causes haemorrhaging.'

'Yup that's the theory.' Peter utters collecting car keys from a rack by reception.

'And his dried up corpse, what do you suppose caused that?'

'Currently no idea but the fact the mayor was so keen on hurriedly closing the case just raises my suspicions even more. There was no need for him to get involved. He doesn't get involved in cases normally. And even further, no next of kin. No family or friend.'

Both policemen run towards the car park, trying not to get soaked from the heavy rain which is now coming down so hard the rain drops resemble that from the sequel to Matrix the movie where Neo takes on the baddy agent towards the end of the film. Both men scramble into a Kia Ceed eco dynamics, cursing as they do so.

Peter starts the engine and activates the windscreen wipers to full and then pulls out of a tight corner with ease. Changing gears swiftly, skipping from gear two to four.

'The fact he has no one in his life is a bit strange, that I completely agree with.' John searches in the dashboard for something.

'Actually it's not that strange, you'll be surprised just how many people are on their own, mostly due to family disputes and an incapacity to socialise.'

'How far is it from the A233?' John turns the light on in the car and examines a paper map splayed across his lap.

'John the sat nav is on.' Peter jests.

'I know but I've told you before, my sense of direction is terrible and relying on a sat nav just makes it worse.'

'It's about 15 minutes, give or take; with this rain probably more give.' Peter affirms still smiling and he places his hand on John's lap delicately. John touches Peter's hand and looks at him with a wry smile.

The car rushes through a country lane with no street lights, spraying rain water over the road verge. A fox dazzled by the car lights frantically scurries away from the side of the road as the car approaches. The car swerves round a bend at about 40 miles per hour – creating an arc of rain water.

'It should be the next turning.' Peter estimates from the sat nav and takes his hand off John's lap.

'I think you need to slow down.' John studies the map.

The car speeds past a sign which reads - A233 next turning.

Both Peter and John sit up in their seats in anticipation.

'It's around where that wooden fence post ends.' Peter instructs, pointing to a wooden fence partly covered in thick bramble. The car pulls up at the end of the fence where damage can be seen, caused by impact.

Both Peter and John get out of the car and close the doors simultaneously.

'This rain is ridiculous.' John mutters as he swings his torch around. It is pitch dark save for an illuminated area over a hill with a few dwellings.

'I think it's starting to ease off now though.' Peter predicts, peering over a fence bordering a field. Cows hurdle up under towering trees, sheltering from the rain.

'Poor things.' He attempts to walk briskly through massive ferns. The rain is just spitting now, to both the men's relief. 'Unusually quiet now.' Peter whispers wiping his brow of accumulated rainwater.

As soon as Peter finishes his sentence, barking sounds travel from the lighted dwelling over the hill.

'Not anymore.' John climbs over the fence avoiding bramble. Both police men have their torches on. Unexpectedly a scurrying in the thick of the bramble gets their attention.

'Poor wildlife, we must be scaring them half to death.'

They both saunter through the bramble which comes up to their knees. Eventually they come to a small clearing.

'What do you suppose this clearing is for?' Peter points to the area in question.

'I think it's just a boundary before the woodland ahead. Borders like these are good for wildlife.'

'How did you know there is wood...? Don't answer that.'

'Good old map.' John taps his folded map.

'How about this, what's the purpose of this?' Peter points to dark zinc like slanted sheet that is bordering a swamp.

'That's to keep the newts in.' John says.

Peter surveys further along the boundary and can now make out a lone cow standing in the middle of the field.

'How come that cow is not hurdled up with the rest under the trees?' Peter gives John a puzzled expression.

'That IS strange.' John changes direction slightly and starts to walk towards the cow which appears to be stood still. Peter follows. The rain has completely stopped now.

Both men continue towards the cow, Peter eventually glances back at the other cows hurdled at the boundary of the field. The cows stare at the men with piercing huge eyes. It's as if the cows are frightened for them, almost as if the cows are trying to warn both men with their eyes, through telepathy.

The lone cow is facing away from them and continues to stand dead still.

Peter picks up a branch from the ground and snaps it in half. It makes an audible cracking noise despite the dampness. The cow remains motionless.

'Spooky.' Peter mumbles.

'Very weird.' John agrees.

Both men's hearts are beginning to race as they continue to walk cautiously now towards the cow. They both take deep breaths and slowly exhale, remembering their training as police officers to keep calm in stressful situations. Neither of them would have thought they'd have to one day use their training for a motionless cow in a field.

'Hey!' Peter shouts partly to scare the cow into motion and partly to break up the tension in his heart. The cow remains motionless.

Not long after he shouts, a strange humming noise starts.

'What's that?' John asks.

'It's getting louder.' Peter reaches to cover his ears.

Both men drop their torches which roll for a bit in the clearing and they hold their ears, squeezing their faces in pain. They both fall to their knees into the floodlight given off by the flashlights. The humming is akin to a road drill with more intensity but less bass.

Peter starts to bleed from the nose, John is now very frightened. Peter does not realise that he is bleeding from the nose until a drop of his blood falls on a big blade of grass. 'What the hell.'

John now gapes with concern at Peter whilst reaching to touch his behind and when he brings his hand back to the light it is covered in blood.

'What's happening Peter?'

Both men gawp at each other with terror in their eyes as the high pitched humming continues. They give each other a discerning look which contains a mix of emotions but definitely a predominant one of regret from lost time and missed opportunities to say or do certain things. The humming noise is now deafening and blood starts to ooze out of John's left ear as more blood flows from Peter's nose. Both men reach out for each other, holding hands. Strain appears on both their faces whilst they hum to themselves in an attempt to comfort one another, but mostly to block out the intense unfamiliar humming noise. It has taken on a whole different piercing tone, vibrating the ground that the both men are now coiled up on.

Peter remembers lyrics to a song by the Manic Street Preachers called 'The intense humming of Evil.' He reconciles his fate but not before deciding to look up at the cow mysteriously standing alone in the field. A lone tear of blood trails from Peter's left eye. He can just about make out the cow's face. It has turned to fully witness the men coiled in distress on the ground. As Peter decides to give into the overwhelming sense of peace that threatens to consume him, he takes one more glance at the cow and swears the cow is smiling at him as she stares with piercing large bovine eyes.

Chapter 13

Lloyd is sitting on the porch to the cottage smoking a cigarette; he peers intently at some undergrowth in the distance and takes a long drag of his cigarette. He pulls his mobile phone close to him and checks it for a signal. The signal is almost zero; he flicks the phone with his finger and turns to continue looking at the undergrowth. Something scuttles in the shrub and a fox appears, it stops and stares at Lloyd for a while before casually strolling off into some other undergrowth. Lloyd checks his phone again and sighs at the single signal bar.

Without notice a humming noise replaces the sound of crickets and gradually increases in frequency. Lloyd remains seated and continues to stare at a particular shrub – the same shrub the fox had appeared from earlier.

Lloyd puts a finger in his right ear and shakes it vigorously in order to stop a deep itch. It is overwhelmingly soothing. He recalls his mum often doing the same with her ear and he particularly remembers as a young boy seeing the immense satisfaction on her face. Funny how certain traits are carried over through genes.

When he was a young teen he used to think that in sexual intercourse being penetrated was so much more pleasurable than doing the penetrating. Just like the sensation you got from sticking something in your ear; it was the ear that got the pleasure not the implement. The chosen implement did not get any satisfaction at all and he likened the implement to a penis. As a gay man albeit he was versatile, he certainly enjoyed the bottom role over the top.

"If society did not have such a taboo about anal penetration and stimulation, mankind could be enjoying sodomy. I mean hello... G spot. Jeez Lloyd stop it already with thoughts on anal sex."

Lloyd shakes his head, smiles to himself and continues to pay attention on the shrub with even more intensity than before.

The humming continues and Lloyd reaches for ear plugs he has in his pocket and pushes them into both his ears. He has always carried ear plugs as cutting out sound helps him think analytically. His mind flashes back to the time he used to go clubbing and how eventually as he aged he had to use ear plugs to withstand the deafening music. When he forgot them, his ears would ring for days afterwards. He could only imagine what it must be like to suffer with Tinnitus.

A reverberating ripple engulfs the shrub Lloyd has been staring at and this ripple of sound waves expands, enclosing the cottage and Lloyd.

Chapter 14

Caroline sits in a cafe in surveillance mode, checking out someone in another cafe across the road; the person she is monitoring is Ryan. Her phone rings and she answers it immediately, whilst inspecting around her. She never knew being a reporter would make her this paranoid or perhaps it was still remnants of the rape experience hanging over her like a shadow of apprehension.

'Yes, Caroline..........sorry what?'

Caroline listens intently to the caller.

'Do you know how it happened?'

Pause.

'Uh huh – And you say he died in a wood?'

Pause.

'Okay – thanks for informing me. Please let me in on the autopsy report once it's confirmed.'

Caroline hangs up the phone and holds her head; she then pulls her hair with both hands and then gazes at Ryan who is still sitting at the cafe speaking to someone on the phone. She swigs the last of her drink, leaves some money on the table and marches across the road to the cafe. She walks straight up to Ryan and sits herself down.

Ryan is startled whilst still listening to someone on the phone. Caroline remains seated and smiles.

'Erm...I have to go, I'll call you later today.'

Ryan switches his mobile off and Caroline smiles cheekily at him.

'Can I help you?'

'Yes you can.' Caroline replies, still smiling.

Lloyd ambles through woodland paying particular attention to the ground and placing his feet cautiously. He calls out with a stage whisper.

'Jaime, are you here?'

Lloyd stops in his tracks and listens intently. Nothing but deafening silence.

'Jaime.' Lloyd calls out this time a little louder.

He continues to walk, a dull light beckons in the distance and he strides towards it, brushing aside overgrown shrub as he does so. Some evidence of something having been through where he is walking, creates some sense of a path.

'Jaime!' Lloyd calls out again with slight irritation this time.

He smiles to himself as he recalls horror movies where people are alone somewhere in the dark, often a woodland or basement and calling out loudly, continuously. The audience watching would always think how stupid, shut up! You're just alerting the killer to where you are.

Here he was doing the exact same thing albeit he had faith there was no killer; perhaps some unknown danger but certainly no one brandishing round a machete or chainsaw or knife.

He takes in a deep breath and calls out again 'Jaime.....if you're here please answer me. It's me... Lloyd.'

'My name is Caroline, I'm a reporter.' Caroline reaches out her hand.

'Hi.' Ryan reluctantly puts out his hand for a shake.

'How can I help you?' Ryan scans around, particularly at the waiter and people who are sat next to them. He watches their facial expressions to see if he can decipher what it is they will be thinking at this moment, and how very wrong they will be. The misjudgements of a heterosexual world.

'I think you may be investigating the same thing that I am and was wondering if you'd like to join forces?'

'And what would be the thing we're both investigating?' Ryan retorts releasing his hand from Caroline's.

Caroline smiles and leans in towards Ryan.

Ryan cautiously pulls away a little.

'Something sinister encompasses this little town and you know it as well as I do.'

'Oh, and what would that be?'

'Oh cut the crap Ryan, you can trust me.' Caroline pulls back and ironically folds her arms.

'How do you know my name?'

'I just told you I'm a reporter – it's a small town. Connect the dots.'

'Okay, you have my attention, but why should I trust you?'

In some way Ryan already trusted her, he was taken in by her smile, something cheeky but innocent and kind about it. He had always been inspired by strong, beautiful women ever since being obsessed with The Bionic

Woman starring Lindsay Wagner. He adored this fictional character learning most of his values and belief systems from her, whilst also being thrilled to the bone when she used her bionics to kick butt. He adored Caroline's confidence instantly, more so because he subconsciously knew she had had to fight for it. He envied her ability to seize opportunities as they arose. It was something he was aspiring towards as a private detective.

'I may be the only person you can trust, except Peter that is.'

'Hmm you've obviously done your homework –but like you said, small town. I'm presuming your meeting with the mayor did not go very well then?' Ryan asserts as he clasps his hands together and smiles at Caroline.

Caroline smiles. 'He's a cliché of a deceitful politician with no integrity. I believe he's covering something up and I intend to find out what it is, but I also believe I'm out of my depth and so joining forces will be a good thing for both of us.'

'What makes you think I'm out of my depth?' Ryan unclasps his hands.

Caroline smirks and raises her eyebrows. 'Really….you want to do this?'

Ryan glances down at the table and then back up at Caroline.

'Okay, okay what have you got?'

'You, like me, think that the guy in the car accident was a weird one, something does not sit well with you.'

'I happen to have been on the road, in traffic jam because of that accident and yes there was something off.'

'Was there a humming noise?'

'Now that you mention it there was a quiet humming, almost like when your ears pop or when you stay quiet and can hear a consistent frequency or like the ringing in your ears after a night of clubbing.'

'I wouldn't know about clubbing, but I guess it's rare to find a gay guy that has not been exposed in some way to clubbing of some description.'

Caroline gives Ryan an even broader smile.

'So you've done your work no need to show off.' Ryan bends down to scoop out a digital camera from a satchel at the side of his chair.

'I did take some pictures on the day of the accident which may be of interest, wanna see?'

'You're quickly taken in.' Caroline adjusts her seat to get in closer.

'Or perhaps I'm just a good judge of character, besides like you I've done my work on you and I've decided no need for me to be wary.' Ryan winks at Caroline.

'Okay, the wink is creepy even for a gay guy.'

'Do you want to see these pictures or not?' Ryan retorts and presses a button to begin the photo roll.

'Too much light, hang on a second.' He adjusts the brightness of the screen to compensate for the brightness of the day.

'Hold up, what's that?' Caroline points to the road side in the picture.

'It's probably just the light reflections again.' Ryan adjusts the camera and moves it around but what looks like a smudge still remains in the picture.

'Hmmm, not sure what that is – could it be a distortion in the frame due to the weather...perhaps?' Ryan doesn't believe his own explanation.

'You don't believe your own explanation, do you?' Caroline quizzes Ryan.

'Is it some sort of ripple on the image? It has to be something wrong with the camera, there has to be some kind of explanation. There was no mention of anything strange in the papers. Not that that is a surprise.'

Caroline moves in close to Ryan and whispers. 'What do you mean? You think there are things being covered up as well don't you?'

'Well something is definitely strange about this town, although can't put a finger on it. And I'm not just referring to the superstitions either.' Ryan replies also with a lowered tone.

'The idea that there has to be two of things or places due to the parallel universe, which every local seems to believe exists, has to come from somewhere.' Caroline moves her chair back.

'Also do you feel a little paranoid when the locals look at you?'

'Yes, something unnerving and can't put a finger on it. But then again it may just be a habit we hone as part of our profession.'

'Maybe…....Anyway I must go meet..'

'Peter.' Caroline interjects.

Ryan smiles. 'Well Caroline you have been simply resplendent.'

'Well, thanks Ryan….. very sweet of you.'

'Don't get used to it, if we're going to be working together then I reserve the right to be ruthless if need be.'

'Oh and ditto Ryan, Ditto.' Caroline gets up and shakes Ryan's hand.

'Seriously though thanks, I do appreciate it.' Caroline bows her head and then walks off. She stops, walks back and slips a card to Ryan.

'My number.' She winks, chuckles and struts off again.

Chapter 15

Peter sits in a library; three people sit in the far corner of the large room he is in. For a small town, it is a big library with a sliding ladder, that stretches further to books stacked up high. It resembles the library in the Harry Potter movies. Peter scans a newspaper from the sixties using a Lupa TV Magnilink X Reader 19, a section about the cemetery and the fact there were a lot of baby deaths due to an epidemic, is in bold in an article. As he scans the paper, he is impressed by the high tech scanning equipment present in a local library in a small town. He doesn't remember seeing one of these magnifying instruments in any library in London.

"There are other b…" The little girl's muttering shoots through his neural cortex as he moves the magnifying glass over the article. "There are other…. what? I'm going to need to speak with Contiana about this experience. Was it some kind of vision?"

He has always been open to all sorts of possibilities. He has experienced all kinds of things that could not be explained easily and so had learnt not to be too quick to discount something based on so called lack of grounding in reality.

"What was reality? So many things cannot be explained and there're so many magical things in nature for instance that don't necessarily follow the laws of science sometimes. So why not visions? Nothing is wrong with my brain so far as I'm aware. Throughout history there are accounts of people having visions. What was the little girl trying to tell me?"

His mobile vibrates, making him jump. The library is so quiet that the sound of the vibration easily penetrates the soundless void. Peter quickly takes his mobile out of his pocket and at the same time peeks to see if the three people in the room have been distracted. All three of them are staring at him. Were they already looking at him? They keep their gaze for a fraction of a second more and then return their attention to what they are reading. He is thankful they don't do this in a synchronised fashion, because that would be too weird.

He checks his mobile and smiles at a text from Ryan.

'Meet me at the Taverna – the one closer to the library you're in just to be certain. I've got some interesting news for you.'

Peter pulls away from the Reader 19, and gets up as quietly as humanly possible; he does not wish to be stared at again by the weird library musketeers.

He walks out of the library with some haste. He had promised himself to be less urgent about things in his mind, as this was to help him with anxiety and depression. But this time, he does not wish to slow down his mind and his sense of urgency. After a text highlighting 'interesting news for you.' Peter believed it warranted breaking a new replacing habit – just this once at least.

'There are so many unanswered questions for Contiana.' Ryan reports as he waits for Peter to fill the hired car up with diesel.

'Yes I agree completely.' Peter admits, partly distracted as he spies on the attendant in the garage store. He pulls his card out of the machine mutters and pushes it back in.

'God, why is it taking so long for the card to register?' He regards the attendant again. This time the card registers and requests for his pin. He hesitates for a brief second recollecting his thoughts, as he needs to remember the pin. He has used different passwords and pins for his electronic accesses – he believes this helps prevents scam artists accessing his various accounts. The trouble is he has extra difficulty remembering the passwords or codes for each thing. He has written all the various codes on a piece of paper at home and some he has put on his phone as fake telephone numbers. If he was really stuck, then he would access his phone to find the code. Peter delicately puts in his pin and after a few seconds the machine accepts the card, he removes his card at the prompt.

Peter gets in the car not bothering to take his receipt as he has stood at the petrol pump far too long for his liking. He knows he is making efforts to stop being so urgent about everything but the petrol fumes are too much. He has never understood how some people like the smell of petrol.

'Contiana is expecting us and she's prepared for further questions.' Peter starts the ignition, and puts the car in gear. As he drives out of the garage he takes one more peek at the attendant who appears busy with other customers – he has not noticed him once. He wanted to be sure he was not getting paranoid. Certain people in the town had so far been suspiciously eerie. It was a relief that this garage attendant had not paid him any attention.

'All good?'

'Yes, yes everything is fine.' Peter decides to keep this part paranoia to himself.

'So you're sure you can trust this reporter…..what's her name again – Caroline?'

'Yes that's right and yes funnily enough I do – one of the things that help me in my job is my judge of character.'

'That's good to know, should come in useful.' Peter acknowledges as he turns a bend in the road.

'So this experience you had on the street. Wanna run it by me again…..properly.' Ryan scratches the shallow depression behind his knee.

'Wouldn't you rather wait till we got to Contiana's so you don't have to listen to it over again?'

'No, I would like to hear it whilst we drive over to Contiana's... if you don't mind.' Ryan responds, still scratching behind his knee.

'Well…..I was walking down the street, not drunk and hadn't done any kind of drugs not even poppers.' Peter looks at Ryan with a partial smile.

'And, a girl was walking alone towards me – she wore a lilac dress, I guess I should be glad it wasn't red huh?'

'What do you mean?'

'Haven't you noticed how in the movies, in certain scenes, the little girl always has on a red dress to signify something? "Schindler's List." and "Don't look now." being prime examples.'

'No, I can't say I have.' Ryan replies. He has stopped scratching his leg but inspects it occasionally, somewhat perplexed.

'Anyway, the little girl was walking towards me whilst only paying attention to the ground, and for some reason I felt tense. I felt as if something bad was about to happen. I often get anxious for no reason but this was different, I felt extra sensitive, all my sensories were on high alert. As the girl walked past me she looked up and whispered, there are other...something, didn't get the last word. Think it began with a B. A loud noise distracted me, and when I looked back the girl had vanished.'

'Could she have turned a corner?'

'She could have, more than likely that's what happened but it's what she said that's important here, right?' Peter raises his voice and his eyebrow towards the end of the sentence.

'Of course, course, wonder what she was referring to?'

Lloyd continues to walk through dense shrub, avoiding brambles and nettles the best he can. Up ahead in the distance is the silhouette of a person standing as still as the atmosphere they're in. He treads heedfully towards the figure, but this time decides not to call out. As he approaches, he sees that the figure is facing away from him. He is almost within touching distance, and he picks up the courage to call out again.

'Jaime.' He whispers as he reaches out his hand to touch his shoulder.

'Yes Lloyd, I hear you......just be quiet for a while will you.'

___

Peter, Ryan and Contiana sit outside in her porch with a large jug of lemonade. It is sunny out, and in Britain you make the best of the sun where you can, no matter what.

'So I help you with, what can?' Contiana smiles cheekily.

Ryan wonders why the Yoda display of words in the sentence, but decides it's probably just a white witch thing.

'We have some more questions.'

'Let's hear them.' Contiana replies pouring lemonade into glasses.

Contiana had always been a strange child – she was the only child of hippie parents. They brought her up to appreciate and respect nature, but whilst they communicated freely with her and were always truthful, they did not lavish her with affection except on themselves. They were madly in love with each other and having a child did not distract them from this doting love. Although she knew she was loved she always felt like a bother to them somehow, always disrupting their passionate moments on the sofa or that stealing kiss in the kitchen whilst they both made dinner. She liked their love but to her it was also suffocating and at times she caught herself resenting them both for not giving her more attention. She wished she had a brother or sister to play with.

The one thing that consoled her was her different view on reality, when she turned six years old she had a strange experience that she never forgot or shared with many people. She was standing in a glade observing nature around her, and the ground started to vibrate, emitting a humming noise. At moments she felt as if she was one with the ground, and all around her, and she knew in that instance that the reality everyone sees and observes is not what it seems. It was like she became so present she was on a molecular level with all around her. She felt it in her waters and bones so to speak. And she would never let anyone tell her different.

This was one of the reasons she dyed her hair every so often, for one she liked being different and it made her feel like a new person each time, but mostly it was her way of expressing her rebellious side which was defying reality as others saw it. She took delight in tentatively exploring hues of spicy intense red, pastel pink dip dyed tips, mahogany with honeysuckle highlights, auburn and sometimes even mossy green.

Contiana became a nurse as she loved caring for people but after only practising for a couple of years she decided to explore alternative medicine and soon afterwards got interested in modern witchcraft.

She believed reality was distorted and we only experienced parts of it. In her teens she believed the brain was incapable of sensing reality as it really was – but as humans evolved they would get to truly see and become extremely powerful creatures. For now, most humans were scared to fathom the idea of such power and so subconsciously people kept within comfort zones and dared venture out into unknown realms of reality except when on magic mushrooms, but not Contiana.

'Why did you advise that we go to the cemetery?' Peter starts.

'Well, I was hoping you'd tell me.'

'What d'ya mean?' Ryan ensures the Dictaphone is on.

'I had a premonition that you both go to the cemetery, I have no idea why.'

Both Peter and Ryan acknowledge each other's bewilderment.

'You mean to say you just had a vision that we visit the cemetery but you have no idea why?'

'Precisely what I said.' Contiana utters before taking a sip of her lemonade. 'Right now I advise that you drink your lemonade before this heat warms it up – it's better cold.' She winks at both the men. They stare at her still perplexed.

'You tell me what you observed at the cemetery and we'll all try to figure it out together – How about that?' Contiana suggests smiling.

Both men obediently take a sip of their lemonade, if only to change their perplexed faces.

'Well, I've had a few weird dreams, and a possible vision whilst wide awake.' Peter starts.

'Interesting…....please more.' Contiana leans in and waves her hand as if ushering for a taxi.

'I've had some disturbing dreams about crying babies in a Cemetery. I saw something on a tombstone that I saw in a dream, and yesterday I saw a little girl in some kind of vision who tried to tell me something.'

'Okay one thing at a time Peter dear – I'm not that good a witch.'

'In the dream, there were crying mutilated babies in the ground – Ryan and I noticed when at the cemetery that there were a lot of babies buried. On research we can see there was some sort of epidemic, but why the weird dreams?'

'Perhaps the babies are trying to tell you something?' Contiana proposes before taking another sip of lemonade.

'You're asking him?' Ryan retorts.

'We often have the answers; we're just too scared to embrace the vast possibilities.' Contiana answers as she inspects one of the crystals on the table. She looks up from the table and continues.

'Maybe there was an epidemic. Some people, some witches I should say can predict the future of babies and sometimes those futures are bleak and evil. Actually, there is an old wives tale that says when a feeding baby grabs the breast with great vehemence, that baby's soul has been on earth many times before and it is feeding for all the other souls long past gone. Souls that have been on earth the most times are more prone to evil.'

'What exactly are you trying to say?' Ryan bellows.

'The babies were killed because their bleak futures were seen.' Peter says from a place of divine wisdom.

'Who killed the babies, and even more importantly who covered it up?' Ryan is dismayed.

'The portal openings to other dimensions allows for certain witches to see into the future.' Contiana adds solemnly.

'This just gets weirder and weirder.' Ryan exclaims checking the Dictaphone.

'Can people go to the other side?' Peter asks whilst having a flashback of the guy at the reception desk staring at the wall.

'Yes.....but there are consequences.' Contiana replies.

'What kind of consequences? Would dehydration be one of them?'

'Yes.' Contiana simply replies.

Peter holds his head in his hands. 'Jaime went to the other side didn't he?'

'Yes.' Contiana enunciates holding the crystal on the table.

Peter deliberately pinches his forearm and takes a glimpse at Ryan. Both men observe each other in a mix of shock and disbelief.

'This is all a bit much to take in.' Peter proclaims letting go of his forearm. 'How do we even know we're in the right dimension? Things have been pretty damn strange in this town or village or whatever it is that we're in.'

'I know how it all sounds, and how you might feel but reality is purely our perception, and our brains are limited. I knew this from an early age. I can however assure you both we are in the dimension we're supposed to be in.' Contiana declares holding her crystal.

'Do you know where the portals to the other side are?' Ryan is still in bewilderment.

'The portals are not consistent in one place they show up randomly.'

'Okay that helps...not.' Ryan mutters shaking his head.'

Contiana bursts out laughing. 'That must be the most common Yoda used expression.'

'What...... oh never mind.' Ryan realises now that Contiana must be a Star Wars fanatic.

'Can you sense someone that is on the other side even though you can't see them?' Peter continues to hold his head. He remembers smelling Joop in his room and the crumpled note that was in the waste paper bin.

'In rare cases you can, only where there is a strong bond. There does have to be something........ never mind.'

'Something?' Ryan interjects.

'It's nothing, the bond is most important.' Contiana asserts.

Peter is consoled. Ryan touches Peter's hand compassionately. Peter lets him. Contiana notices and smiles.

'So all this has something to do with Quantum Physics?' Peter slowly moves his hand away from Ryan's reach.

'Yes, you remembered.' Contiana smiles and takes another sip of lemonade.

'There are proven theories emerging that back up parallel universes. Not necessarily windows into other worlds but from studying the molecular atom in detail, scientists are able to decipher that we're all waves of energy. Unfortunately, the irony is it's hard, very hard for our brains to comprehend it all as our perception is limited, as I've said and this of course gives cynics a field day.'

'How do you know so much on the subject?' Ryan checks the Dictaphone.

'I've always been fascinated with molecular theories, ever since I was a child. In some ways that's what got me into witchcraft, believe it or not…..modern witchcraft anyway.' Contiana smiles at Ryan.

'Does the name Joanne Faber mean anything to you?' Peter asks.

'No not particularly. Why?'

'We saw a tombstone with that name on at the cemetery.'

'Is that significant?'

'Well, in some ways yes as I dreamt about being in a cemetery and observed a kind of symbol and some letters. That same symbol was by Joanne Faber's tombstone.'

Peter grabs a pen and draws the symbol on some scrap paper on the table.

ꝺb

'It looks just like this.' Peter gives the symbol he's just drawn a cautious look.

'Some kind of ancient letter, yes I believe that is one of the letters that was discarded from the English alphabet.' Contiana states as she turns the piece of paper around.

'Really?' Ryan studies the symbol.

'Yes, there were some letters which were only used temporarily in the alphabet and then discarded; like the Ampersand, the symbol still used today to shorten the word - And.'

'This one?' Ryan grabs the pencil and draws &.

'Yes, that was once part of the alphabet and there were others, I believe this symbol you saw is one of them.' Contiana conveys with certainty.

'That is fascinating, what do you suppose it means?'

'What was the age on the tombstone?' Contiana asks.

'Oh, erm, it was eighteen something to nineteen seventy something.' Peter replies.

'Possibly a nice rounded figure.' Contiana expels.

'Pardon, oh I see.' Ryan quickly realises what she means. 'A hundred years old, not many lived to that age in those days.'

'Indeed, unless you were a witch.' Contiana mutters at the crystals on the table.

'You think Joanne was a witch?' There is no judgement in Peter's words.

'Not sure, I'm just contemplating.' Contiana responds.

'There was something I never showed either of you.' Ryan gets out his sophisticated camera and switches it on.

'Oh…..how come?' Peter frowns.

'I just needed time to assess everyone, sorry, old habit. I've always kept some stuff back just in case. Please don't take it personally.' Ryan considers Peter.

'I'm sure Peter understands.' Contiana mentions.

'Something weird showed up in a picture I took when I witnessed the car accident.'

He shows the digital picture to both Peter and Contiana.

'Do you notice anything strange with the picture?'

Contiana and Peter scrutinise the picture and Peter is the first to point to the strange blur on the edge of the snapshot.

Contiana pulls gently on her hair. 'What's that?'

'That's what I couldn't explain. I showed it to a reporter this afternoon over coffee.' Ryan declares.

'Oh.' Peter exclaims.

'Her name is Caroline Fletcher and I think she'll be a good ally.'

Peter ignores the additional comment and continues to scrutinise the picture.

'Hang on a second.' He turns the picture around and looks again and he can just make out something that looks like ♉.

'Anyone else notice?' Peter asks.

'Well, you think that looks like the symbol in your dream?' Contiana now combs her hair with her fingers.

'Yes, don't you?' Peter cross-examines.

'It does kind of look like it, but what on earth would that mean and why show up in the picture in the first place?' Ryan is perplexed.

'Perhaps Lloyd will be able to help.' Contiana says with a smile.

'What – has Lloyd been in touch?' Peter tries to contain his excitement.

'He has indeed – he called to say that he might be on the brink of something.'

'On the brink of something?' Ryan repeats more puzzled than ever.

'Who speaks like that?' Ryan adds.

'Lloyd does.' Contiana responds smiling.

'I see.' Ryan rejoins, feeling slightly ashamed of his criticizing behaviour. 'Where... when do we meet Lloyd?'

'Well he said he'll call me this afternoon and was expecting his call by now.' Contiana responds turning around to check the clock on the wall which mimics a smaller version of a vintage grandfather clock.

'When did he make contact?' Peter wells up with sure hope.

'A couple of days ago.'

'Did you mention that I'm here and looking for Jaime?'

'No I didn't, to be honest I didn't get a chance, he wouldn't shut up.'

'He was excited about his discovery and kept saying it will change everything, everything we know about reality.'

'What do you suppose he meant by that?' Ryan interjects.

'He did not have time to say, but was insistent that we meet as soon as possible.'

'What time did he say he'll call?' Peter tries hard not to be over excited.

'He should have called an hour ago.' Contiana replies attempting to conceal her disappointment.

Lloyd stands patiently waiting for Jaime to turn around and pay him attention. After about a minute which felt like an hour, Jaime turns around to face him. He appears gaunt, with prominent cheekbones. He has unkempt hair and stubble, and his bloodshot eyes are clumsily situated in black rings. He stares at the woodland floor.

'You shouldn't have come here.' Jaime says with sadness.

'Why, what do you mean?'

'We aren't supposed to be here. There are consequences.'

'I can remember the precise spot where I came in.' Lloyd declares.

It doesn't matter, it doesn't work like that, the portals don't remain in the same spot.'

'That's just great, he's gone missing too.' Ryan retorts.

'What is wrong with you today?' Peter expresses concern.

'I'm sorry, that was insensitive of me.'

'Yes it was.' Peter adds and turns towards Contiana.

Contiana smiles whilst looking at both men.

'I got some interesting facts about missing people today from the library.' Peter says, desperately trying to change the subject, and the awkwardness that has begun to arise in the air.

'Never mind that, tell Contiana about the experience with the little girl after leaving the library.' Ryan says with enthusiasm.

'Oh, what experience?' Contiana places her hand on one of the crystals.

'Well it was pretty strange, a little girl walking past me on the street turned around and tried to tell me something. I got the words (there are other......) lost the last word to a racket made by a truck.'

'And you have no idea what this last word could have been?'

'I was distracted by some crazy truck driver and when I turned back around she was gone. I think it was a word beginning with the letter B.'

'And that happened in broad daylight – you were awake?'

'Yes I was awake – I was walking along the street.' Peter affirms.

'I think you may have seen a spiritual doppelganger, and you're beginning to sense the other dimension.' Contiana declares, stands up and goes out into the back garden. She leans into a large plant pot, and meticulously moves soil with her hands to unearth a big crystal which she then delicately cradles, as if holding a baby and brings it back to the table with her.

Both men visually engage Contiana waiting for her to explain both her words and actions.

Contiana carefully places the large crystal on the table next to the others, and she takes a moment before responding.

'Ever since I was a child, I have sensed that reality is translatable. Most children, if not all, sense this but this ability is eventually lost due to closed minded parents. I decided to hold onto mine and not let it go. My parents helped with this in the way they brought me up.'

'When you say reality is translatable, what exactly do you mean?' Ryan asks keeping an eye on the Dictaphone.

'Precisely that. Like I said before our sensory organs and our brain use is limited. Note that I say the word "use." Our brain capacity I believe is infinite but we only use about ten percen…'

'Ah, now see that is a myth.' Ryan interrupts. 'There is no scientific evidence to back that up.'

'Pfft, a simple play on words.' Contiana utters.

'The word "use" is the problem – of course any mention of us not understanding the brain completely threatens most scientists and doctors but I'm afraid that's still the case. We don't fully understand the complexities of the brain.'

'Albert Einstein was the one that mentioned the 10% brain use – albeit that may have been misinterpreted. The fact still remains; we have limited understanding of how the brain works or indeed how we use it.'

Both men are baffled by the knowledge that Contiana has and the eloquence with which she passes it on.

'You only have to look at mental illness – depression and anxiety. We're completely in the dark about it. Excuse the pun. Depression continues to be the number one killer in the world, over all, with mostly men taking their own lives. If we were so on top of the brain, surely we would have figured out a definitive way of eradicating this chronic invisible mental illness.' Contiana smiles at both men.

'I did read an interesting article recently about how inflammation in our bodies causes depression in people. Apparently, this inflammation that tends to be high in a third of people that experience depression, affects the serotonin in the brain; but then again other scientists claim that there is more to depression than just reduced serotonin in the brain. So I agree with Contiana, when it comes to the brain we're all just walking around in the dark with a match stick for light.' Peter reciprocates.

'Profound.' Ryan mutters.

'Good word for the brain.' Contiana says and smiles again. 'On a serious note one can see why people would be addicted to anti-inflammatory drugs.'

'Hopefully we've opened up our minds a little – who's to say that we observe all of reality as it is? How do we know, given our limited perception that we see all that there is?' Contiana challenges, whilst caressing her crystal.

'Like I said earlier, Quantum Physics; the new science in my opinion, is proving that there are alternate realities, parallel universes and dimensions. Various accounts of unexplained happenings in the world cannot be explained with today's science, and our limited ways of thinking. Unfortunately, most people cannot, and will not take comfort in not knowing it all so to speak. Fortunately, a few of us do take comfort in knowing that we DO NOT know.' Contiana takes her hand off the crystal and reaches out for Peter and Ryan's hands.

Both men place a hand each in the hand closest to them on the table.

'Woh!' Ryan exclaims.

'So warm, your hands are almost hot!' Peter helps Ryan find the words to explain.

'We're all just pure energy.' Contiana conveys smiling as usual.

'You mentioned spiritual doppelganger, what's one of those?' Peter catechizes.

Ah, as previously mentioned, children often sense alternate realities. But on top of this some children are extra sensitive and will have a spiritual doppelganger..... a kinda replica that guides people in other dimensions. I believe I have a spiritual doppelganger.'

'And you think the girl I saw on the street was a doppelganger?'

'Yes I do and she was trying to tell you something, something important.' Contiana speaks with an ancient wisdom.

Peter stares into the distance recollecting the afternoon when he met the little girl on the street.

A screeching loud noise dominates all sound as the brakes to a truck are applied and machinery in the back of the truck is flung around adding to the cacophony. The little girl turns around and speaks but it is only drowned in the mind splintering noise.

'Please now tell me about your research at the library.'

Peter is jolted out of his memory and has to replay his mind to figure out what Contiana has just said. He inspects Contiana's hand where he still has his clasped, secretly hoping that it doesn't combust.

'It was some interesting facts on missing people in the world.' Peter stares at the clasped hands on the table.

'One that immediately got my attention is that globally, 607 people go missing every single day without a trace.'

'Really, where'd you get that statistic from?' Ryan is intrigued.

'Google.'

'I also learnt today that you are called a Skiptracer.' Peter adds, looking at Ryan.

Both Contiana and Ryan give Peter their best inquisitive faces.

'It's a term used for people that find missing people.'

'There's actually a term used to describe it?' Ryan checks.

'Yes, apparently so; it just goes to show how common it is for people to go missing.' Peter adds.

As Peter speaks, he acknowledges it should give him some sort of comfort knowing how common it is for people to go missing, but frankly it doesn't. He has never understood the sentiment of comparing yourself to others in order to feel better. Like someone saying to you when you're depressed, to cheer up as things could be worse. You could be that person – with no legs or that person - with terminal cancer. These kinds of comments from people never consoled him, as he never compared himself to others. He was a positive person generally and knew to be grateful about things in his life, but when he was really down in the dumps comparing himself to others was not what made him feel better. He fully believed that at the end of it all we were all on our own separate journeys – comparing yourself to others was just plain stupid in his opinion.

'Any other interesting facts?' Contiana now removes her hands from the hands of her guests.

'The missing white woman syndrome. Apparently there is an ingrained obsession in society over the "Damsel in distress." And so there is extra attention given to white women, possibly with blond hair, who go missing.' Peter divulges, feeling the warmth in his hands.

'That's interesting – another fact to show how much crap society imposes on us all.' Ryan blurts out, whilst registering the warmth in his hands.

'Societal influences do have a lot to answer for; especially for us gay men.' Peter adds.

'It certainly does – said the white witch as she carefully rearranged the crystals she had on the table.' Contiana says, and moves the large crystal to the side and chuckles to herself.

Peter laughs quietly and eventually so does Ryan.

'What are you trying to say? That we're trapped here?' Lloyd is not sure of the emotion that has conjured up in him.

'Not necessarily trapped, but let's just say we won't be returning in the same molecular structure as we came in if we're not careful.' Jaime now peeks up at Lloyd. His eyes are tired and somewhat cold and lifeless – like a shark's.

'But don't worry I've been observing the portals closely, and I may have a plan – I think I know which one will be the right one to go through – The timing though has to be precise.'

'Well that's a relief.' Lloyd expels air that had gotten caught up in his upper lungs on hearing Jaime's initial revelation.

'How about phoning someone?' Lloyd fishes his phone out of his pocket knowing that he is late with phoning Contiana. He presses the numbers hurriedly with primal excitement.

The laughing trio are interrupted by Contiana's mobile phone ringing – the ring tone is strangely or perhaps not so strangely 'Woodstock by Joni Mitchell.'

'Hello.' Contiana answers with a bright smile that has indistinguishably followed on from laughter.

'Hello.' She repeats. She listens intently, slightly furrowing her eyebrows as she does so.

'Hello.' Contiana pronounces again this time squinting her eyes.

She takes the phone away from her ears and holds it away from her with concern.

'Couldn't hear anything?' Ryan stares at Contiana.

'Nope, but not only that, the distortions were strange.'

'How'd ya mean?' Peter cross-questions.

'It just sounded strange, distant.' Contiana adds.

'That won't work.' Jaime returns his gaze to the woodland floor.

'Hello, can you hear me?' Lloyd ends the failed call and reluctantly looks at Jaime. 'You tried calling me, didn't you?' He recalls answering his phone in the cabin and not being able to hear words, only strange distortion sounds.

'Yes.' Jaime utters.

Lloyd drops his face in despair and panic. 'So what do we do?' He returns his attention to Jaime attempting to reconfigure some positive contours to his face.

'We need to be patient and we need to remain very observant.'

'What are we looking for?'

You'll know, there'll be a humming noise and you will have some weird sensation, almost as if there's a mild electric current running through your body.' Jaime adds.

'God, this just gets weirder and weirder.' Lloyd narrows his already slit eyes.

'There are three locations to which I know of, we may need to seek a fourth. Believe it or not the portals operate on some kind of mathematical formula.'

Lloyd listens intently, unable to come up with words to follow in the conversation, if at all it was ever a conversation.

'Luckily the locations are all close together – must be all part of the formula.' Jaime adds.

'I was able to make some kind of contact with our dimension.' Jaime has a flashback of the crumpled note in the bin.

Lloyd continues to remain baffled; his neural cortex just can't cope. He stares at Jaime with a wishing trust that all will be okay, and that Jaime knows exactly what he is doing.

'There is a pattern, but that pattern varies which makes it a bit more complicated. I'm fairly convinced that I've cracked the pattern, and that the formula is correct. But of course I am still being cautious, as a 5% doubt could be what makes the difference between life and death.'

'That's comforting.' Lloyd says, taking a deep breath.

'It's all we have, and I have studied it meticulously – I believe I have cracked it.' Jaime adds for reassurance. He is aware how his stats may not be all comforting, but then life is never all comforting.

'You must have known that where you came in was saf...okay. You wouldn't have known though that to come into this dimension was easier than it was to get back.' Jaime says.

'I'm sure I saw a fox and a blackbird come in through the portal.' Lloyd says without much conviction.

'You may not have seen the same fox and blackbird that went in.' Jaime declares.

'Also, if the wrong portal has been entered getting back, you only last a couple of minutes before...swivelling up...literally.' Jaime adds.

'What do you mean swivelling up?'

'It's almost as if your molecular structure becomes devoid of water.'

'This is just nuts! Why Clophill?' Lloyd bellows in agitation and confusion mixed with despair.

'That one I can't answer. I do know that the portal can sometimes spring up on you. That's how I got here; I certainly didn't willingly go through a portal.'

Jaime has a flashback to being in the wood scared with two men closing in on him whilst he hide in a cotoneaster shrub. One minute hands were reaching for him and the next he was tumbling down a small hill into a brook. The opening portal had more than likely saved him. He had literally fallen down the rabbit hole!

'This makes you very brave indeed whilst also helping with the puzzle of how these windows open and close.'

'Trust me it had nothing to do with bravery.' Lloyd gapes at the ground and mutters to himself. 'More like stupidity.'

'Could it have been Lloyd?' Peter interrogates with anticipated hope.

'Possible.' Contiana checks her mobile phone.

'You said the distortions where distant.' Ryan checks.

'Yes I had a similar call not long after Jaime disappeared. I was almost certain it was him but all I got were strange distant interferences.'

'Are we being contacted by the other side?' Ryan tries to sound serious.

'Precisely what I was thinking.' Contiana places her phone down on the table.

'How very Poltergeist.' Ryan adds.

'Jaime was trying to contact me – I know this for certain now. I didn't want to say anything because it seemed crazy but I smelt Joop in my room and also found a crumpled note with Jaime's hand writing on.'

'Really?' Ryan is in complete bewilderment.

'Yes, definitely – he's trying to get in touch with me. He's alive, God he's alive.' Peter starts to cry.

Contiana reaches for Peter's hand and holds it firmly allowing Peter to sob.

Ryan blinks his teary eyes.

'You will see him again – I know this for sure.' Contiana reassures him.

Peter wipes his catarrh and tears on his shirt sleeve. Contiana gets up spritely to find him tissue. She returns to the table swiftly and Peter takes the tissue and blows hard into it. He continues to wipe his eyes with his shirt sleeve which now looks like there's been an after party of a slug gathering. He retains the tissue for his runny nose.

'I'm sorry.' Peter pleads still wiping his eyes.

'There's nothing to be sorry for.' Ryan reaches for Peter's hand and gently holds it. 'Like Contiana says we'll find him.'

'Thank you Ryan.' Peter blows his nose again.

'Now back to the babies at the cemetery.' Contiana tries to cause some distraction from the present mood.

'What about them?' Peter wipes his nose relentlessly, he is conscious of bogies.

'We need to ascertain how they died and why so many of them, and why you had the dream you had.' Contiana adds with a sombre face.

'You think it's some kind of conspiracy?' Ryan starts to wonder why he even bothers questioning anymore.

'I didn't say that – I just put out some theories to explore with is all.' Contiana clarifies.

'You said that some witches could see into different universes, and so predict the future of a child – Do you know any other witches like you?' Ryan grills.

'I only ever knew one but she's passed away now and she is...was a lovely soul.' Contiana responds with a smile that masks a bittersweet sadness.

'May I ask her name?' Peter now pockets his snotty tissue.

'No she was not Joanne Faber.' Contiana says immediately.

'How did you know I was getting at that?'

'It's obvious, besides wrong era. This friend of mine was called Hannah Coleman.'

A humming noise interrupts the conversation; it appears to come from the distance. It sounds like a radio station frequency attempting to re-tune.

'What's that?' Ryan scans around.

'I have no idea.' Contiana answers.

'I think it's getting louder.' Peter starts to feel his pockets.

'Contiana closes her eyes for a few seconds, and then opens them. 'We need to get out of here now.' She vocalizes with a stoic face. Both men stand up abruptly. Ryan grabs the Dictaphone.

'Happy to drive?' Contiana checks with Peter.

'Yea sure – what's going on, have you experienced this before?' Peter questions as he scampers to the exit.

The humming begins to intensify. A flock of black birds scatters out from some trees nearby.

'Quickly to the car!' Contiana shouts, still retaining the seriousness. The men know that something is wrong. Contiana not smiling is abnormal. They start to run.

'Quick, quick, quick.' Contiana grabs the door handle to the back seat, swinging the door open and gets in.

Peter dashes in and starts the engine, grateful that he did not lock the car.

Ryan shimmies in after him on the passenger side. Now it's as if the ground is vibrating with the humming noise.

Peter hustles the gear just as a deer runs out in front of them; everyone jumps in shock. The deer takes a look at them and then runs off towards the bridge.

'Follow that deer!' Contiana commands.

Peter reverses the car picking up dirt with the back tyres as he does so, and then changes the gear swiftly and turns on the radio in the car. He hopes to pick up news on the weather, but all he hears is crackling interference. He adjusts the dial, and in the same breath changes the gear and floors the accelerator. The car spins towards the bridge.

Contiana glances back at her abode as they speed off. A muntjac makes an appearance from the wood and scurries towards them going into some nearby shrub.

The car approaches the bridge and Peter slows down.

'No, no don't slow down – we haven't got time!' Contiana shouts.

'Are you sure?!' Ryan shouts.

'Yes I'm sure, floor it.' Contiana asserts and hits Peter's thigh hard.

'Oww.' Peter exclaims but presses down on the accelerator pedal nonetheless.

The car propels forward mounting the bridge which buckles immediately.

'Oh god!' Ryan says grabbing hold of his seat belt.

The humming noise begins to lessen as the car speeds over the bridge. Peter lets out a breath he has held for the duration of time whilst going over the bridge. Ryan loosens his grip on the seat belt. He has pulled on it so hard it has caused a strain on his neck.

'I think we're out of the woods – no pun intended.' Contiana declares smiling.

'So you want to tell us what that was all about?' Ryan continues to drive but slowly. 'You obviously knew what that was and have even experienced it before.' Ryan continues. The question wipes the smile off Contiana's face.

'What did you say?' Jaime ogles Lloyd sternly.

'Nothing, nothing, let's just figure out a way of getting out of here.' Lloyd turns away from Jaime's piercing eyes.

'We have to find another potential portal; the formula becomes a bit more full proof then.' Jaime begins to walk to their left towards strange incoming fog.

'Do we have any idea of time?' Lloyds inspects his surroundings.

'It's dusk, that's all we need know.'

'Is everything the same, solid ground, trees, leaves, air?' Lloyd calculates where he treads.

'Yea, pretty much.' Jaime replies.

'Pretty much?'

'Yes, pretty much..........the only difference is subtle, very subtle. Come with me.'

Jaime walks hurriedly towards a small glade and finds a bare spot on the grass and cups his hand in the soil. He lifts his hand up and then lets the soil filter through his fingers.

'Do you see it?' Jaime asks.

'What am I looking at?'

'Concentrate………just take your time.'

Lloyd looks on and takes a deep breath as he does so.

'Nope, I can't see anything.'

'Perhaps it'll be better if you pick up some soil, and carefully let it spill from your hand.'

Lloyd opens his hand, and grasps a handful of dirt. He lifts the soil up in a fist, and then slowly releases the tension in his little finger. He watches the soil spill from his hand and eventually exclaims.

'Is the soil dropping weirdly?'

'You see it?'

'It's dropping slightly slower than it should, as if gravity is slightly out of kilter?'

'Something like that yea.'

'How weird.' Lloyd watches the soil drop as if in a trance.

'I honestly didn't know anything about this, well not in this reality anyway.' Contiana declares with quiet assurance.

'What does that mean?' Ryan is now slightly agitated.

'I knew, well kind of knew about this, that this would happen. It came to me in a drea...well a trance.'

'You knew that we would be caught up in this strange humming occurrence?' Peter pulls the handbrake up.

'Yes, I did...why has everyone forgotten I'm a witch all of a sudden?' Contiana retorts.

'I'm sorry; of course, it's not unbelievable that you would have a premonition about this.' Ryan gets out of the car.

Contiana also gets out of the car; she leans on the hood of the car and surveys the direction that they have driven from.

Peter alights slowly; he ambles a little then drops to the floor and sits down in a part lotus position. He picks up leaves from the floor, and he drops them to the ground watching them fall and some waver with the slight wind that is in the air.

Ryan walks over and sits gently down next to Peter. Contiana glimpses at both men and returns her gaze to the road.

'This is some kind of surreal nightmare...literally.' Peter flicks the last leaf off his hand.

'You're not wrong.' Ryan about manages to expel from his lips.

'Why here?' Peter urges quietly towards Contiana. 'Why here in Clophill? Why are there windows to dimensions here, of all places? What's so special about Clophill?'

'Well there is some theory that passageways into other parallel universes are opened if two souls that were never supposed to cross paths do cross paths.' Contiana proclaims walking over towards the men.

Both men look at her now with mastered perplexed expressions.

'Certain people are not supposed to meet..., in this life anyway. It ruins the cosmic order of things.' Contiana adds.

'Then the universe is exceptionally rubbish at managing things huh?' Ryan pronounces.

'I guess the universe never envisioned advancement of modes of transportation we now have.'

'It's our advancement in technology to blame?' Peter tries not to roll his eyes.

'Well not to blame – it's just that our advancement in technology has sped up too soon, not in par with our humanity.' Contiana sits down next to both men on the ground. 'There is a universal order to things and once this is interrupted we have consequences, often dire consequences.'

'Well it's just irresponsible for the universe to put all this on the human race. The human condition is fucked!' Ryan says.

'Not that we are being over dramatic or cynical or anything.' Contiana comments with a smile.

'For centuries, human beings have repeated the same mistakes, basically we don't know how to be human, or to be a being. It's not cynical it's just plain fact.' Ryan retorts with a complete stoic face.

'Our brains don't have the capacity to see the full perspective – we're limited in our understanding and ability to see the full picture and that's our only failing and that is what it is, it's supposed to be that way. We just have to trust that it will all turn out well in the end. The universe has a balancing plan and whilst we may not see or understand it. We must have faith, for in that will we have peace.' Contiana continues with innate wisdom.

'We all have, well some of us anyway, intellectual brains that can't see beyond what is in front of our eyes.' Ryan adds.

'You have to admit it does add to the drama and excitement. It's all Yin and Yang, balance is the key. There's a time to use our intellectual brain and there's a time to push reason to the side and just have faith.' Contiana adds still smiling.

'I guess the next thing you're going to say is that the universe has an ultimate plan and that it's greater than personal love for one another.' Peter adds solemnly.

'On the contrary – love is everything. It's just that we humans confuse love. Love happens on faith mostly. It becomes a problem when we try to intellectualize it. We often confuse attachment for love. In lots of ways love is like quantum physics, there is no observing the atom.'

'Can we get back to our intellectual brain – how do we get Jaime back? Presuming he's definitely gone or been sucked through a portal into another dimension – sounds crazy even hearing me say this but hey.' Ryan puts his hands up. 'I'm completely out of my depth here.'

'You need to get Caroline onboard.' Peter announces.

'Yes, I know.' Ryan mutters.

'The reporter?' Contiana enquires.

'Yes.' Peter affirms. 'We need all the help we can get.'

'Does she buy the whole parallel universe thing?'

'She will, she's liberal enough.' Ryan replies.

'Then let's get her onboard. A nice even yin yang number.'

'What... Oh.' Peter stands up.

Hard rain splatters down in a cul de sac, creating petrichor. A few cars are parked on a kerb because space for parking is sparse. A straight couple argue outside one of the houses. The front door is ajar, and a little girl stands quietly next to it unnoticed by them. Behind the girl are flashing coloured lights which emanate from the windows. Loud disco music fills the atmosphere. Caroline hurriedly walks past in an attempt not to get too wet. She arrives at her porch and turns in the direction of the couple.

'You know your little girl can hear every word, you should probably quit arguing now to save scarring the girl anymore than your consistent parties have already caused her.' Caroline turns to her door and brushes the water off her arms. The two people stand staring at her, after a while the lady walks to the front door and puts her arm around the little girl.

'Oh and whilst you're both at it you may want to tell your guests to move their cars in case a fire brigade vehicle needs to come through.' With that Caroline slams her front door shut.

'Honestly some people shouldn't be allowed to have kids – they should at least have to pass a parenting test.' Caroline talks to her cat as it comes running up to her meowing her little head off. Caroline picks her up and strokes it as she saunters to the fridge. She grabs a small bottle of beer, puts the cat down, and opens a cupboard. She retrieves cat food, opens the tin and empties it into a bowl.

'There you go Snuffles.' She strokes the cat some more as it snuffles all over the food.

She ambles into the living room and tenders to a plant that is by the window sill. She pulls some of the dead leaves off it and admires the plant. She walks over to a sideboard and grabs a laptop and then sits on a bar stool that is next to a mini bar. She turns the laptop on and sets the bottle of beer down. Her doorbell rings.

She walks over to the front door carrying her bottle of beer with her. She opens the door to find it is the neighbour who was arguing with his girlfriend on the road.

'You know, you should mind your own business.' The man pouts.

'I am, if I wasn't I would have said you both don't deserve to have a child.' Caroline retorts without batting an eyelid.

'You are one cheeky bi...' Caroline throws the remainder of her beer over his face mid sentence. The man reaches for her and Caroline moves back whilst putting her hand out and grabs him by the forearm pulling him towards her and in one swift motion she slams the door on his arm.

'I would hurry along now to your missus mister before I report you for assault.' Caroline slams the door shut as the man rubs his arm and winces in pain.

She returns to the fridge and grabs another bottle of beer and places the empty bottle down by the side.

'Coming here and causing me to waste my beer.' She tuts and strokes Snuffles some more just as she finishes off the last of her meal.

She marches back to her laptop and spins it around and types. The doorbell goes again.

This time she grabs something that duplicates a baton and flounces to the door. She swings it open. 'Seriously, you're messing with the wrong perso...'

Ryan and Peter stand in the doorway.

'Hi.' Ryan says with raised eyebrows. 'You always answer your door with a baton?'

'Is this how you knew you were not….. well, in a weird place that wasn't home?' Lloyd is still fascinated with the sand dropping from his hand.

'Yes kind of, other than there was no one around.'

'Oh, well that would kind of give it away.'

'Also I can't seem to get out of this wood.'

'Okay that's not good.'

'Well actually it's fine - leaving here would only be a distraction. The answer for getting back to our reality is in this wood. No reason to leave the wood.' Jaime forces a smile.

'And how long have you been here? Do you know?' Lloyd now throws the remainder of the sand out of his hand. The gravity novelty has worn off.

'Probably a few weeks.'

'Well that can't be right; you've been missing for months.' Lloyd responds swiftly. 'But then time is not the same here.' Lloyd drops his gaze as he answers his own mystery.

'Well I guess it's one good thing - feeling like you've been here for longer must take its toll.' Lloyd utters with some upbeat.

'Follow me. I managed to find somewhere, somewhat comfortable for us to rest.' Jaime starts to walk confidently towards denser wood.

Lloyd follows without a word. Sometimes in life nothing can be said and in this situation he had done extraordinarily well to speak as much as he had, because quite honestly he was dumbfounded by the whole state of affairs.

Chapter 16

People yell out, some in lullabies, selling their fruit and vegetables. The louder and coarser the language, the better to attract the customers. Sometimes a little humour goes a long way in getting attention. So the occasional innuendo or euphemism does not go amiss. Wednesday is market day and its billingsgate galore.

'Fancy a bit of jiggy jiggy tonight, then get your hands on these jiggy asparagus people, only £5.99 a bunch.' One of the male trader bellows.

'Have you seen anything more orange than these oranges?' States a female trader somewhat subdued as she knows there is no way that statement beats the one by the asparagus trader.

'Comfort yourselves by holding one of these, ladies - £5 a bunch.' Shouts another female trader selling bananas.

'Fuck meat, get some fish!' Shouts a female fishmonger that fits the stereotype of a butch lesbian.

Then there is the generic. 'Why buy tomorrow what you can buy today!'

In a corner of the market square a dog barks frantically. The owner holds its lead and is pulling but to no avail. The dog furiously continues to bark at a rotund man walking past. The man is Donald. He is on his mobile phone.

'I don't see the relevance quite frankly, not one bit.' Donald scorns at both his mobile and the barking Alsatian whilst walking past cautiously.

'What would make someone check for elastin on a cadaver in the first place?'

Pause.

'Uh huh, okay got it. I really must go now.' Donald terminates the call and is now out of reach of the Alsatian, but the dog continues to bark at him with the occasional growl. The owner inspects Donald then the dog and then Donald.

Donald speed dials.

'Yes, can someone check to see what the function of the protein around the walls of arteries is? Give me a synopsis of what would happen if there was too much or too little of the stuff.'

With that Donald terminates the second call and continues to walk through the market square. He spots another dog in the distance, this time a terrier mix. He decides to walk in the opposite direction. In his psyche he is aware this all has to do with him raping a dog when he was younger, but he does not wish to have a conscience about it. He skedaddles, managing to avoid people, and if not nudging them out of the way with his fat.

"Who says being overweight doesn't have its advantages." He smiles to himself.

He squeezes into a car, parked on a single yellow line and takes his time in the vehicle. He turns the radio on and listens to the local station as he starts the car, and drives off.

'Two police officers are found dead in a field after a strange storm.' The news presenter relays in a posh voice. *'The circumstances around their death are uncertain at this time, but forensics think it might be electrocution from lightning.'* The news presenter continues.

Donald smiles as he turns the car at a junction and into a dementia care home.

Chapter 17

Reflective shiny dew droplets withhold their position on the leaves of trees and shrubs. Golden sunlight filters through the woodland. It is unusually quiet, no birds singing or chirping. Along a border, a hand stretches out of a concealed cave, pushing dead leaves aside that have accumulated at the entrance overnight. Eventually Jaime appears out of the cave and stretches. Soon after Lloyd comes out with a solemn look on his face.

'At the cemetery, that was you wasn't it?' Jaime questions out of the blue.

Lloyd drops his gaze. 'Yup guilty, I was just curious.'

'Hey, no need to justify or apologise, I'm glad you did.'

'I was kinda hoping this would all be some kind of fucked up nightmare.' Lloyd scrutinises his environment.

Jaime acknowledges him but does not utter a word; he starts to pick berries from the shrub.

Lloyd stares at the clouds in the sky.

Jaime peers at him whilst picking the berries.

'That is another give away that we're in a different reality.' Jaime focuses on a punnet proving difficult to pluck.

'The clouds are all upside down?' Lloyd is not sure about the words he has just uttered. He is not sure how else to describe it. The clouds appear upside down; they all have flat surfaces at the top and extend out into mushroom like puffs at the bottom.

'Yep, I noticed it myself on the second day, so well done.' Jaime forces a smile.

'Yea me.' Lloyd remarks sarcastically as he continues to gaze at the clouds in amazement.

'So we are effectively reversed somehow?'

'It would seem so, the strange gravity pull I guess agrees with that hypothesis.'

'So water draining in a sink will drain the opposite way too I guess....anticlockwise as opposed to clockwise.'

'I guess so, I never really thought of that, but that makes sense now you mention it.'

'So weird, it's a good thing I was into "What the bleep do we know." Otherwise I reckon I would be freaking out about now.'

'You read that book too?' Jaime puts on a more genuine smile.

'I did and watched the film - mind blowing stuff.'

'You think there's some universal plan why we're both here?' Lloyd starts to pick berries too.

'Who knows.'

'It's so funny how the older you become you realise you don't know jack shit about anything. That's wisdom essentially, owning that you don't know jack shit.'

'It would make a great book title - "You don't know jack shit!"'

Both men laugh, albeit nervously and this gives them some momentary much needed relief from their literally juxtaposed reality.

'So what's the plan - how do we find the other portal you were talking about?'

'I put some sticks down to mark off areas, and I'm pretty certain the area we'll be exploring today will have the other portal, as it hasn't shown up in the other contours.'

'Sounds promising.' Lloyd transfers the berries he has picked, to an area on the ground where Jaime has placed his collection of punnets.

'Let's have breakfast and we'll go see.' With that Jaime drops a blackberry in his mouth. 'It makes a massive difference having company.' Jaime reaches for another blackberry.

Lloyd glances at him whilst munching on a blackberry but does not say anything. He wants to say something, something comforting, but he can't think of anything so he decides to be quiet. Apparently his company is comforting without words.

Chapter 18

Donald plods down the hallway in a dementia care home. On the walls are Monet style paintings of flowers and of people fishing from bridges and boats. Donald guesses that the choices of paintings are to appeal to both sexes.

"Some people would think it was sexist, some stupid people, queer people perhaps."

The colours in the home are soothing and he wonders if the colours have also been conscientiously selected. The carpet has no patterns which he learnt on a previous visit was to help people with advanced dementia not trip and fall. Patterns on the carpet made them think there were obstacles in their path. Everything is homely and welcoming until you inspect the ceiling and notice the lights. They are fluorescent lights, encased in ugly cumbersome rectangular fixtures. The kind you'll find in a hospital.

"A bit of effort to change the light fittings would have made all the difference. Surely I can't be the only one to think this."

He walks into a living room where an elderly lady sits in an armchair staring out of a window.

'Hi mum.' Donald pulls up a chair to the side of her and plonks himself down. Putting himself on autopilot so as to follow the usual routine when he visits.

'What you looking at?'

The old lady continues to stare out the window with no change in expression on her face.

'You have quite a pleasant view there huh, I do wonder what you see though - do you see something else? Do you even appreciate the scenery you have?' He is now slightly off his usual script.

'GRANDMA!'

Donald turns around; a boy about eight years old is cuddling an elderly lady on another arm chair across the room. A woman who has walked in with the boy lets go of his hand so he can fully embrace the old lady.

Donald fidgets in his seat, and adjusts his crotch. His mum gives him a sinister smile.

'You're aroused aren't you?' Donald's mum squares up to him now, it appears she has all her faculties, almost as if a few moments ago her staring gormlessly out of the window was all just pretence.

'What do you mean?' Donald scans around as he responds to his now seemingly compos mentis mum.

'You're aroused by him.' His mum gestures with her head to the little boy and his gran mum.

Donald leans into his mum and whispers with some vehemence.

'What are you saying? Why would you say something like that? I have never touched a child in that way, EVER. Why would you say something like that?'

'But you think about it.' His mum continues to eyeball him. 'Don't you? You think about it.' She grabs hold of his arm and nudges him to look at her as he has now looked away.

'YOU THINK ABOUT IT DON'T YOU?!'

This time it's Donald's turn to grab hold of his mum's arm.

'Listen here you old bag, stop it now. You don't know what you're talking about, you're delirious, and you're in a loony home in case you'd forgotten.' Donald scans around nervously to ensure he hasn't been heard.

With that his mum turns away, and resumes her normal stance of staring out the window.

'Why do you have to go and be such a nasty bitch of a mother?' Donald whispers.

Donald takes a deep breath and composes himself as he peeks at the little boy from the corner of his eye. He watches his mum attentively as a tear rolls down his face. It's as if he never truly saw his mum before. He wipes the tear and stands up. Before leaving, he bends a little closer to his mum, as much as his extra weight will allow him, and he holds her arm.

'You have no idea how much fighting I do, no idea at all - every day is a battle.' Donald says quietly. 'Here…it makes sense really, here is where I decide to confide in you.'

Donald takes one more peek at the little boy before walking away.

'You wouldn't have to fight on the other side.'

Donald stops in his tracks. What could his mum possibly mean? Is she aware of the dimension opening and if so how on earth would she know about it? He turns around and walks back to his mum and sits down.

'What do you mean?'

His mum continues to stare out the window.

'You wouldn't have to fight on the other side. There'll be no need for you to suppress it son.'

Donald inspects the living room cautiously.

'What do you mean? How do you know about the other side?'

His mum continues to stare out the window.

'That's where I go.' She whispers and smiles whilst continuing to stare into oblivion.

Donald sits as if paralysed. He stares at his mum and for one brief moment senses unadulterated love, the unconditional love that only exists between a mother and her child. A bigger tear rolls down his cheek.

'He he Ha ha ha ha ha ha, stop it granma.' The little boy in the corner is being tickled.

Donald does not look round; he holds his composure and continues to look at his mum as if meditating on her face. Another tear rolls down his cheek.

Both Jaime and Lloyd walk through woodland; Jaime is in lead, following sticks that he has placed down to show them the way.

'This is all some kind of weird voodoo bullshit isn't it?' Lloyd scrutinises the woodland floor for the sticks. He wonders how Jaime is able to find them, as it all appears camouflaged to him.

'You say that because we're black?'

'No because it's some weird voodoo bullshit.'

'Why us, why are we here?' Lloyd continues, trying desperately to dispel the anxiety that is threatening to cripple him.

Jaime observes him, and is intuitively aware. The anxiety had gotten hold of him for the first few days. He remembers an unusual dream he had last night.

'I had the strangest dream last night.'

'What about?' Lloyd takes in a deep breath.

'I got on the bus with Rosa Parks; I was back in time and got on the bus with Rosa Parks. Can you imagine?'

Lloyd stares at him.

Jaime is pleased he remembers the dream as it's good enough distraction as any to help alleviate the anxiety that is about to engulf Lloyd.

'I got on the bus with Rosa Parks, knowing it was her. I think I purposely went back in time to meet her. Other black people were on the bus mostly women and we all sat at the back of the bus. There were a couple of white people, if I remember rightly, mostly men.'

'Some elderly camp guy in the front with the driver got on the intercom and said - There are an awful lot of ghouls here today. And the white folks sniggered to themselves. It was obviously some derogatory term as a couple of black ladies sighed. I got up and walked over to the front of the bus. A fat man stood in my way, blocking me from advancing any further, and I pushed him hard, and he tripped down the stairwell to the bus and smacked his head hard on the door. There happened to be two shots of liquor in small tumblers on the dashboard of the bus. I grabbed them and threw them in the face of the old camp guy and the driver. - Isn't that the strangest dream?'

'It sure is - I wonder what it all means, two shots of liquor, very random.' Lloyd is interested and appears to be deciphering the dream.

Jaime is pleased his distraction has worked, albeit he was just as excited about remembering the dream.

'I do feel sorry for white folk sometimes, it must be a drag being constantly reminded about how inhuman their forefathers were.'

'Yea and it annoys me how some black folk continuously play the racist card when it's not warranted. The poor white folk are continuously treading on eggshells.'

'But then again racism does persist, so what to do?'

'What to do indeed.'

'Here it is.' Jaime stops in front of a tree trunk, which appears to have been two trunks that have fused together.

'That's apt.' Lloyd traces his hand along the fused join of the trunk.

'So what do we do - become genuine tree huggers?' Lloyd forces a smile, an attempt to conceal the anxiety that is beginning to rise up in him again.

'Something like that yes.' Jaime inspects the back of the tree.

'It's like a perfect fusion right?' Lloyd continues tracing his finger along the trunk.

'Now we wait.' Jaime checks around.

'What are we waiting for exactly?'

'The right time.'

'How will we know….. ?'

'Okay, okay, I don't have all the answers, stop with the questions!' Jaime bends down to feel the ground.

Lloyd stays quiet.

'Sorry Lloyd……….I didn't mean to shout at you, you've effectively risked your life to find me and that was insensitive of me.'

'That's fine, we're all on edge. The truth is Jaime I actually felt like crying then.'

Instantaneously a surge of vulnerability flushes over Lloyd and he craves sitting down to cry his eyes out. And he would have liked nothing more than to be held tightly by Jaime as he sobbed. But he forces himself to swallow the grief that is about to overwhelm him.

"What good would crying like a baby do? No good at all. So get a grip Lloyd, just get a grip!"

'I'm cool.' Lloyd manages through the lump in his throat.

'There'll be a humming noise and a slight vibration on the ground.' Jaime glances around again.

Both men sit down on the woodland floor in silence for about five minutes.

'Why do you think Clophill of all places? Why here?'

'Have no idea.' Jaime does not take his eyes off the ground.

'Some theory explains that some of us mess with the universal laws without knowing, and this may have something to do with it.'

'Mess with it ho.......sorry.'

'That's okay.' Jaime replies. 'Apparently certain people aren't supposed to meet in this lifetime, and if they do, then that affects the parallel universe paradigm.'

'Do you believe that?'

'I don't know what to believe in all honesty, not anymore anyway. Contiana told me that when I visited her last.'

'She said that sometimes, rarely, people plan too much and force things to the point where it is completely out of alignment with how things should be. She went on to say that people are expected to primarily go with the flow and trust and have faith in the universe to deliver what we need. Unfortunately, society and the advance of technology has meant that pushing and forcing the hand so to speak has been exacerbated beyond all measure, and this has in turn fucked with the electromagnetic energy of the universe field.'

'Wow, that's a lot of hippie stuff.'

'I know, I know, you asked.' Jaime simply replies.

'It still doesn't answer the question why Clophill? What's so special about Clophill?'

'Well I did come here to research witchcraft perhaps that has something to do with it. I did uncover some odd findings.'

Lloyd stares at Jaime waiting for the rest. 'And?'

'Well, there was the cemetery and the babies. There were a lot of babies, and there were no records of an epidemic, none that I could find anyway.'

'Contiana said that some witches could foresee the life of babies, by somehow manipulating the portals to parallel universes.'

'Are you saying what I think you're saying?' There is pensiveness in Lloyd's voice.

'Yes it would appear the babies were killed, I think to prevent them becoming some kind of evil incarnate. If you think about it, if you knew a baby was going to turn out to be Hitler….'

'I knew there was something weird about this town.' Lloyd remarks as he scratches his arm.

Jaime watches him scratch. 'There's certainly some hidden conspiracy going on. The superstition over having two places of the same name and the involvement in the parish council.'

'What do you mean?'

'Almost the whole town attend the parish council, surely you noticed.'

'Well, I was mostly isolated in a small house in the wood after you disappeared.'

'The town holds and hides a deep secret. Whether this has anything to do with the different dimension openings is not clear but I will bet it's all interlinked somehow.'

'It's like friggin Wicker Man.'

Suddenly a slight tremor in the ground vibrates through their backsides.

'There…..you feel that?' Jaime stands up off the bed of leaves they have been sitting on.

'Is that it?' Lloyd lifts up off the ground as well, his anxiety returning with full vengeance. He scratches his arm furiously now and Jaime has concern in his eyes.

A humming noise starts and Lloyd holds his head with one hand and the other he places on the fused tree trunk.

'Are you okay?' Jaime reaches for Lloyd's arm and holds him.

'My head is banging to that humming, don't you feel it?' Blood starts to spill from his nose.

'No I don't, damn it we both have different openings.' With that he grabs Lloyd's arm and pulls him. 'Quick follow me, this will be dangerous for you.'

'What do you mean? Why just me?'

'Follow me, quickly.' Both men start to run as the humming intensifies. Lloyd holds his bloody nose and runs after Jaime.

'Run, run as fast as you can!' Jaime snaps, thinking he sounds like something out of an adventurous fairy tale.

Both men run faster though the woodland, jumping over fallen branches and shrub. Lloyd tries to keep up with Jaime who continuously tells him to run faster. As Lloyd picks up speed he scrutinises the leaves on the trees which flutter even though there is no wind.

Caroline, Ryan and Peter sit in the living room of Caroline's semi-detached house. Caroline's cat is curled up in Peter's lap and is purring madly.

'She never takes to strangers normally.' Caroline remarks as she puts down a few more bottles of beer.

'Caroline you mentioned that the mayor may have something to with the accident, and the recent deaths of the two police men in the field.' Ryan mentions pulling out his Dictaphone.

'Yes, yes but I must insist, no Dictaphone.' Caroline points to the recording device.

'For the entire meeting?' Ryan is confused.

'I don't trust or better still know how proficient you are and wouldn't want what I'm about to tell you to end up in the wrong hands.' Caroline utters firmly.

'Fair enough.' Ryan turns the Dictaphone off and Caroline pays close attention, to ensure that is exactly what he does.

'Can we get on with it?' Peter retorts while stroking the purring pussy that has curled up into a ball in his lap.

'I believe a massive conspiracy goes on in this town, and we have to be extra careful.'

'It's too much of a coincidence that the one police man that has information for me is found apparently electrocuted in a field. It's way too coincidental.' Caroline reaches for her beer and takes a swig.

'You said he came across as a man with no integrity…the mayor I mean.' Ryan checks.

'Prevaricates, like any other politician, a fat bully mostly, but I still wouldn't underestimate him. For one he's the mayor, and second he seemed overly callous.' Caroline adds.

'What makes you say that?' Peter wonders.

'Just something about him.'

'What kind of information did the policeman have for you?' Ryan is conscious of his tone. He doesn't want to sound too serious.

'He had a theory that there was some kind of UFO cover up.' Caroline puts her bottle down. 'I know, I know, before either of you say anything - it sounds crazy and totally x-filesy but that's what he said.'

'He believed there was some correlation between the parallel universes, the engrained superstition in the town and UFO's and the Mayor and an elite few were all aware of it and had some kind of bargaining tool to why they kept it between themselves.'

'Where do the dead babies come in in all this?' Peter ponders.

'Dead babies?' Caroline tries to stay composed.

'Yes, in the cemetery there were a lot of dead babies, it appears there was an epidemic but some things don't add up.' Peter states with confidence.

'What d'ya mean?' Caroline grabs her bottle of beer and holds it firmly.

'Well according to the papers the epidemic lasted for a particular period of time. The dates on some of the gravestones don't add up.' Peter announces again with confidence.

'I read somewhere once that it's possible to get a tear in the universe, a tear in the fabric of time and space, is how they put it, and this weird metaphysical phenomenon is called a rift. Is it possible this is what has happened at Clophill?' Caroline takes another swig from her beer.

Ryan has distinct admiration in his eyes for Caroline.

'What?' Caroline blushes.

'Oh nothing, nothing just, well, actually impressed by your knowledge on this stuff.'

Caroline smiles coyly.

'It still doesn't answer the question why Clophill? Contiana said something about people sometimes corrupting the laws of nature, but I just don't buy that.' Peter interjects.

'That's probably where the UFO's come in…. Perhaps?' Ryan mutters.

'It's an impressive puzzle.' Caroline muses.

'It's nice that you all see it as a puzzle, but my partner is out there, somewhere in this fucking magic cube.' Peter fumes.

'Magic cube?' Caroline tries her best to be delicate.

'Rubik's Cube….it was first known as a magic cube.' Ryan declares whilst putting his hand on Peter's shoulder.

'I didn't mean to be insensitive.' Caroline voices with sincerity.

'It's ok, it's not you, I'm just tired.' Peter attempts to smile.

'We all experienced something bizarre at Contiana's cottage, that's for sure.' Ryan notes with his hand still on Peter's shoulder.

Caroline bends down to pick her cat up.

'We had to flee from the cottage and Contiana was especially certain of danger.' Ryan adds scratching his knee pit, the same one he was scratching when in the car.

'Are you okay?' Peter checks with Ryan.

'Yea, yea I'm fine - I just have a bad itch.'

'You were scratching that in the car too.' Peter mentions.

'You might have a bug bite from all the walking around in the wood you've been doing.' Caroline strokes her cat.

'I noticed a USB stick in Donald's office that I would say he was concerned about.' Caroline mutters in response to neuron networks firing in her limbic system.

'What d'ya mean?' Ryan tries desperately to ignore the itch in his knee pit. It has taken on a whole new itching regime. It reminds him of a trip to Africa when he had to take chloroquine to combat malaria. The side effect of that drug was an itching nightmare!

'When I visited Donald in his office, I spotted a USB stick on his desk that he kept putting his hand over. I think our answers may lie there.' Caroline puts down the cat.

'It must be...he must be hiding something.' Caroline adds getting up and pacing.

'Is there any way we can get our hands on it?' Ryan rubs his knee pit into his chair.

'We might have a way.' Caroline says in confidence.

Both Lloyd and Jaime sit down in the grove of an enormous tree trunk gasping for breath.

'Okay, okay what was that?' Lloyd still struggles to get his breathing to normality.

'It would appear we both have different portals.'

'You mean to say that was your chance to get out of here and you didn't?' Lloyd checks with concern.

'Yup.'

'Thank you.'

Both men sit for a while still trying to maintain a steady breath.

'I couldn't just leave you here, not knowing what to do.' Jaime gets up from the comforting bough.

'I really appreciate it.' Lloyd remains seated on the forest floor.

'I do know what we must do but it means splitting up.'

'I was afraid you were going to say that.'

'I'll give you all the instructions and I promise you if you follow them to a tee you'll be fine.'

'Roger that.' Lloyd tries to conceal the sheer fright and anxiety that is overshadowing his psyche.

'I will take you to your portal before….'

'How do you know for sure it is my portal?' Lloyd tries his hardest to conceal the primal fear in his voice.

'I just do, we haven't got time for me to explain. If we miss this opportunity it will be a very long wait before we get out of here. Follow me.' Jaime starts to walk with urgency.

Lloyd follows closely behind.

'What I've discovered is that if not your portal, then blinding headaches and bloody nose. It would appear that everyone has a certain frequency, and you have to have the correct frequency for the portal to work for you.' Jaime moves branches to the side as he walks.

'Of course, I have no idea what happens to you if you don't get out of the vibrations in time, if you're having the adverse effects. I just know a portal exists which does not present the adverse effects, and this will be the one you want to stay put to the end. The bad news is that the portal is in one of two locations.'

Jaime knows precisely what happens to you if you stay in the wrong portal but he chooses not to tell Lloyd. Although he thinks he may already have. Either way why worsen his anxiety.

Lloyd's anxiety takes a nosedive and somersault all at the same time. He collapses to the ground.

Jaime rushes to him and bends down to pick him up.

'C'mon I promise you we'll both be fine, but you need to come with me now.'

Lloyd takes a couple of deep breaths and gets up.

Jaime grabs hold of his face with both hands caressing his hair as he does so.

'We will be okay. I want to hear you say it. We will be okay.'

'We'll be okay.' Lloyd vocalises.

'C'mon.' Jaime commands.

'The spot I'm taking you to is the highest probability - as soon as the vibration and humming start, if you feel a headache then you leave. I will tell you in which direction to run and what to find when you run. I left a marker on the next spot. You can be rest assured that if it's not the spot I'm taking you to right now then it will be the next spot. Got it?'

'Got it.' Lloyd puts on his bravest face.

'We'll be fine, I promise.'

'Okay.'

'Here, you see the marking I put on the tree.' An etching of a Y is carved ruthlessly on the stem of a massive tree with a sizeable buttress. The Y is the size of an open hand.

'This is the mark you want to look for. The tree will be big like this one, and it's only a few hundred yards before you should see the tree. You'll see a wild rose bush next to it. You can't miss it. Please remain calm and run in that direction, if this location does not work. You stand facing that direction in preparation. It is pretty much a straight line, part of the formula. The tree stands out so even if you veer off course you should be fine. You will see it. Okay?'

'Okay.' Lloyd stands facing the direction that Jaime has pointed him to.

'If you get a headache you start to run okay?'

'Yep.' Lloyd stares in the direction that he is to run towards. He stares at the area hard, supposedly trying to make an imprint of the destination in his cortex.

'You can do this; I will see you on the other side. I really must go now.'

'Why a Y?' Lloyd attempts to distract himself from his fried nerves.

'What?'

'Why a Y and not an X, most people would have etched an X on the tree, why did you mark the tree with a Y?'

'I don't know... that's what came to my head... now, large tree, rose bush, Y on tree.' Jaime gives Lloyd a hug.

'Count to two hundred when you start to run, if you need to run.'

'Right, see you later.' Jaime runs off.

'How long would I have to wait at the other location?!' Lloyd shouts.

'Not long!' Jaime shouts back as his silhouette disappears through the wood.

Lloyd stands in the spot as if frozen. He thinks back to when he was a kid playing hide and seek in woodland with friends. He found that experience nerve racking. He hated being the one left to go and find somewhere to hide. He never ventured out too far just in case the others could not find him and he got lost.

As if manifesting his fear, once the others decided to pull a prank on him and they left him in the woodland and went home. Lloyd stayed hid in some undergrowth for ages and ages, what seemed like an eternity before realising that something was up. He eventually came out from his hiding place and picked up the nerve to shout out, and to his utter dismay was met by deafening silence. The same silence existed now, no birds singing, no twigs snapping, nothing but dead silence.

Lloyd starts to make fists with both his hands. He hopes to God that he doesn't develop a headache which tends to happen when he becomes extremely anxious. He wouldn't know then if to run or not.

"But surely the headache to expect will be much more severe." He thinks to himself in consolation. "Besides there was mention of blood running from my nose too, that should be a big giveaway."

Lloyd starts to hum, he does this to break the silence and console himself at the same time.

He thinks happy thoughts and memories as he hums a bit more loudly. He continues to make fists with his hands and does this in succession. He hums with no particular melody or theme; he hums in abandonment, for a moment he thinks his humming echoes; it must be because of the extreme silence he thinks to himself. It's not long before he decides to stop humming as he's now certain there is humming other than his own.

His fists remain fists for a while as he stares ahead and he tries to sense if he has a headache. He thinks he can feel a headache, takes a deep breath and realises it's his imagination. Of course the mind will play tricks, you think headache you manifest headache. Lloyd attempts to remain calm as the humming intensifies. He starts to feel a vibration underneath his feet. It's as if the woodland floor has developed a pulse. The ground throbs underneath him. Lloyd tries to remain calm, observing his neural network for any kind of a headache. He is certain he does not have one. The leaves hanging off a branch in front of him start to flutter. They flutter as if caught in a wind, but not even a whiff of air can be felt. It's as if the atmosphere has congealed. It's the only way he can describe it. It's difficult to breathe. Nonetheless, Lloyd continues to take in slow maintained breaths, and he reaches his hand to touch his forehead, and feels damp on his temple. He wipes the sweat, closes his eyes for a few seconds and in that instance he is certain he can feel peace or what peace would be like. He seldom achieved this when in Yoga classes but he was always amazed when he did. He recognised the feeling.

'I will be okay.' Lloyd whispers to himself.

The vibration and humming carries on and still there is no headache. He wonders why everything is so blurred all of a sudden and realises its reverberations all around him. Then there is a flash.

Chapter 19

From above the town, Clophill resembles one of those mazes, found in cheap magazines where you have to trace something in the middle out into the open. It is a close knit town with stone walls bordering the churchyard, and cemetery, and little wooden fences bordering most of the homes. Some of the houses have thatched roofs all carefully manicured. The houses all back onto one another forcing a close neighbourhood. Most of the roads are in need of repair and the pavements don't look any different. Some of the roads are cobbled; the main one is where the Wednesday market is held. Most of the town's people bring their garden produce to sell, most of the time they do trade by barter. This they believe is self sufficient and they take pride in having a close knitted community where they all watch out for each other.

The town is particularly quiet this afternoon, except for a dog that barks in the distance. Through the cobbled road where the market will usually be held, cheering sounds come from the town hall situated next to the church. The town hall is a decent sized building which appears out of place in the town as it is the one property that has recently been decorated. It is a smaller version of a neo gothic municipal building that stands majestically displaying a terracotta colour similar to burnt orange. It almost passes for a listed building. The grounds are well maintained, with the garden designed so there was always a plant blooming whatever time of year.

The cheering noise is much more audible now. The main door to the town hall is left open and the hall is packed to the brim with people. Donald is standing at the podium situated at the back of the building. The podium is in the middle of what appears to resemble a Greek Pergamon altar albeit a lot smaller.

Again the inside of the building is well maintained. All the benches are pristine and cushioned for comfort. The walls are all painted in calming subtle shades of yellow and big framed aerial shots of Clophill are strategically placed on the walls.

'It is with pleasure that I take in announcing that the sewerage problem is now rectified, as you may have sensed, no more potent odours, especially in the market section of the town.' Donald announces whilst placing his hands on the fancy pulpit that appears to have been designed to withstand the weight of his fat hands.

Everyone cheers and claps.

'I know that it has been a lot to ask you to attend today on market day, but we needed to congregate.'

The congregation fall silent.

'Now, visitors to our town may think us crazy but we mustn't falter to our beliefs and as usual that reminder has to be put out there.'

Everyone in the hall gape at Donald with expressionless faces.

'We have a few visitors in our town and whilst we must make them feel welcome, we mustn't let them undermine us and our beliefs.'

Everyone cheers and claps.

'They're asking questions, by all means tell them what you know, but retain your right to confidentiality. We have old traditions here and they are what bind us as a community.'

Everyone cheers and claps again.

'There are two men and a woman investigating something, help them where you can but don't feel obliged to.'

Immediately after Donald's last word, a crashing noise on one of the windows alerts everyone. People look in the direction of the sound. Another thudding noise unsettles people further, this time it comes from the roof. Confusion and panic start to brew. People talk amongst themselves trying to decipher what is happening. Donald holds on firmly to the pulpit and stares ahead. The congregation all notice Donald staring ahead and they turn in haphazard fashion to the doorway to observe a raven that has flown in, and is perched on one of the empty benches by the door.

Everyone stares with gormless faces. The raven stands still, as if like a statue on the bench and monitors the crowd without blinking. A few people now whisper to one another in quiet tones of disbelief. Then dead silence again, as the Raven turns its head slightly to the left. Donald picks up the courage to shout.

'Shoo!'

"Who came up with the word shoo, is it derived off shoot?"

The raven remains perched on the back rest of the bench, albeit it has now turned to focus on Donald.

'Shoo!' Donald shouts again whilst gripping the pulpit.

Suddenly another thud at the front of the building this time, and a raven smacks the doorway pillar twitching. Donald is put off by controlled exclamation from the crowd. The raven on the bench continues to watch Donald. It's like the raven is trying to communicate telepathically. It eventually turns around facing the doorway, and flies off just as another unknown object hits the roof; everyone glances up with some of them beginning to make their way to the exit.

'Don't panic people; leave in an orderly fashion.' Donald grips the pulpit but with less angst this time. People move steadily to the exit, everyone trying their best to remain calm.

Ryan and Caroline are in Donald's office rummaging around. Caroline searches the desk and in the drawers whilst Ryan inspects a sideboard and cabinet by the wall.

'It was on this desk.' Caroline utters with annoyance.

'Well, obviously he moved it.' Ryan retorts while checking the drawers meticulously.

'What's this?' Caroline picks up what could pass for a bullet from the drawer. She scrutinises it. 'Well, well...Donald likes the white stuff.'

'Pardon.' Ryan is still engrossed in a drawer.

'This.' Caroline waits for Ryan to look up and then acts out snorting on the desk.

'I guess it's not surprising, to be that pompous you need some help.' Ryan remarks and returns to rummaging in the drawer.

'What colour was the USB by the way?

'Black.' Caroline opens another drawer.

'We better hurry up and find it.' Ryan asserts now searching the top of a cabinet; he moves hunting trophies around on the shelf.

'Not to worry they should be a while at the town hall. Victor told me that the meeting should be a long one for them to hold it on market day.'

Ryan's mobile buzzes in his pocket and he hurriedly retrieves it and reads the text.

'Well not according to Peter, they're all coming out of the hall, some incident with birds!' Ryan lifts his head to Caroline with concern. 'We have to leave!'

'Give me a minute.' Caroline closes the drawer and scans the table again.

'We have to leave NOW!' Ryan asserts walking over to Caroline.

'GIVE ME A MINUTE!' Caroline shouts back.

She scans the table lamp with interest, it's a little lopsided and she grabs it and turns it over. She spots an indentation in the base and stuck neatly in the recess is the USB stick.

'GOT IT!' Caroline puts the USB stick in her jeans pocket.

'Quick let's get out of here!'

Both Ryan and Caroline quickly scan the room and move things slightly to ensure that everything is how they found it.

They hurriedly walk out of the office and down the small hall to the exit.

Another buzz alerts Ryan. He grabs the phone, inspects it and puts it back in his pocket.

'Donald is just leaving the hall; he was the last one out.'

'Well, that was easy.' Caroline smiles.

Ryan and Caroline walk swiftly down the street as Ryan makes a phone call.

'Yes Peter we're out and we got it.'

Ryan listens intently on the phone as Caroline nudges his arm to cross the road.

'Alright, meet you back at Caroline's.'

Ryan ends the call.

'Is he okay?'

'Yes, he's fine. Just perplexed by what happened…..apparently ravens were flying into the building and killing themselves.'

'Seriously.'

'Yup.' Ryan mutters as they both disappear round a street corner.

Chapter 20

Jaime sits on woodland floor and scans his surroundings; he has small cuts on his neck and face but otherwise is okay. He puts his hands all over himself, checking his arms and legs and stomach and finally his head. He scrutinises his environment again, attempts to get up but collapses on the woodland floor and sobs like a child. He has never been so frightened in his life. He folds himself up and cries uncontrollably into his folded arms. After a few minutes he peels his tear moistened face off his arms and rolls his shirt sleeves down. He had rolled these up to observe the goose pimples on his arms whilst waiting in his designated portal to get back to his reality. Observing the goose pimples helped him to remain present and control his fear.

He picks up some of the soil and lets it filter through his hands and he laughs out loud. He stands up and again peers around whilst breathing in the air. He takes in a deep breath, as much air as his lungs can take and slowly releases it and a tear traces down his cheek into the crease caused by his smile. He combs his beard with his hand. He's never had a beard before, not this long anyway. He wonders what Peter would think of it. He wonders how Peter is and he realises just how much he has missed him.

He briskly brushes himself down and then shouts out.

'Lloyd!'

He listens intently and calls out again.

'Lloyd!'

He remembers the two men that were trying to capture him in the woods. What were they trying to do exactly? Why were they so threatened by his questions and research? He was going to find out - that was for sure. He had literally been to the other side to escape them. Well timed portal.

'Lloyd!!' Jaime shouts with all the power of his lungs. He shouts loudly as he is sick of silence, he wants all the noise in the world and he doesn't care if it brings peril. He would never have thought he missed noise but he did. He missed noise very much. Listening to dead silence for days, weeks, months will do that to you.

"How long had I been away for?'

'Lloyd!!!' He screams even louder and then coughs.

He scratches his knee pit before walking towards what appears to be a glade. He remembers spending time in a glade with Peter, and how safe and present he felt when he was with him. The glade was their special sanctuary where they went to recharge their batteries, and indeed their love for each other. He walks towards the glade as if drawn towards it and he becomes aware that somehow his walking is different. It's as if he's a lot heavier on the ground and he's exerting a lot of energy to lift each foot off the ground to walk. Like a baby learning to walk for the first time.

'Lloyd!' He shouts out but with a lot less force, he hurt his throat the last time. 'Please answer me.'

He tries to think if the directions will mirror in this reality or dimension. For a second, he wonders if he has ventured through the portal into the right dimension. Could he have gone through into another parallel universe? After all, no one said it was just one parallel universe, not according to quantum physics anyway. The thought befuddles him and he shakes his head.

"I have to believe I'm in the right dimension, I just have to, it doesn't bear thinking about."

'Lloyd.' He calls out again afraid to shout now. He continues to walk towards the glade; a prodigious tree stands majestically at the border to the glade. He quickens his pace now and strides through overgrown cock's foot grass and cow parsley.

'Lloyd.' He calls out again, praying hard and asking and wishing for a miracle. He needs it. He pleads some more. How is he going to live with himself knowing he left someone behind in an alternate universe, not just anyone but someone that actually sacrificed his life to come and find him? How was he supposed to live with that? He couldn't, he just couldn't, not even with Peter back at his side, he wouldn't be able to live with himself and this realisation bothered him, bothered him a lot.

'Lloyd.' This time he starts to cry. The thought that Lloyd never made it through is too much to bear. He wipes a tear from his face as he reaches the giant tree, he puts his hand out and places his palm on the roughness of the bark and caresses it still crying, then he spots something by a groove on the stem. It's a mark, an etching of an X; it's fresh and smells of resin, like it has just been engraved.

'Lloyd?' This time he whispers. He bends slightly to scratch his knee pit and does it this time frowning. He tries to inspect his knee pit but it is impossible. Why does it itch so much? He must have been stung by nettle or something. Without notice, he feels a tap on his shoulder and jumps in fright.

'Hello.' Lloyd has a big smile on his face.

'Oh, thank god, thank god.' Jaime reaches for Lloyd and hugs him tightly, as if only that moment was left on earth. He sobs into his shoulder as Lloyd is a little taller than him.

'I thought, I thought….' Jaime can't speak, he is overwhelmed and puts his head into Lloyd's shoulder and cries some more.

'You thought you'd gotten rid of me?' Lloyd hugs Jaime tight.

'I have to get in touch with Peter, god knows what he's thinking, he must be beside himself.' Jaime tries to break the emotions that are forming between him and Lloyd. He is still with Peter and he still loves him. Whatever it is with Lloyd is infatuation, caused by heightened emotions in extreme circumstances. He was now literally back in reality, and he must return in mind, body and soul.

'Yes of course.' Lloyd pulls back from the hug and smiles at Jaime.

'I would have expected us to be sick or at least feel nauseous. But I feel fine. Are you alright?' Lloyd checks with Jaime.

'Slightly queasy but otherwise right as rain.' Jaime touches his stomach.

'That's awesome, so which direction do you think?' Lloyd takes a deep breath.

'That way.' Jaime points to the left of the glade. A murky pond is immediately adjacent and has a bunch of bulrushes around it. He remembers always thinking the bulrushes reminded him of hairy hamsters pierced on spikes, and acknowledged that he must have a dark and somewhat twisted imagination which suited his chosen profession perfectly.

'Okay, lead the way.'

'This is crazy, we were in another dimension, a parallel universe, and we just came back into our own dimension. How is our brain even coping with this?' Jaime scratches his knee pit again.

'I don't know but let's not dwell on that shall we. Let's just get outta here.' Lloyd asserts.

Both men double up in that instant and puke their guts up, both reaching for something to hold. Lloyd embraces a tree trunk for comfort as he vomits violently down the bark. Jaime however is unable to reach anything in time to grab on to and he squats as projectile vomit shoots out of him. He slumps to the floor after he is sure his innards have all been spewed out of him.

'That's better, makes more sense.' Lloyd wipes his mouth and eyes at the same time.

'Yep, I guess you're right.'

Caroline, Peter and Ryan are back in Caroline's house. They sit round a table paying particular attention to a laptop. Caroline puts in the USB stick they have stolen from Donald's office. She clicks on the removable disk E: and they all wait in anticipation as the disk loads. A lot of subscripts, symbols, maps and coordinates appear.

'What's all this?' Peter questions as Caroline scans the document.

'Is that the symbol we saw in the cemetery?' Ryan points to the ♭ that is next to some drawings and writings.

'It would appear so.' Peter continues to scan the document. Everything is quite small so it's a little difficult to see and make sense of.

'What are these circular drawings with coordinates next to them?' Caroline points to the bold circles on the screen.

'Is that the map of Clophill?' Ryan points to a map which has several bold circles scattered across it and coordinates written next to each one.

'This is all too weird.' Caroline scrolls down on the document.

'What are these symbols, some kind of ancient language?' Caroline points to a series of symbols that are stacked in some sort of table.

The word "test" is located next to this table. The word is slightly bigger than all the other words in the document.

'What the hell is all this?' Caroline says with real concern in her voice.

'It's certainly foreign whatever it is.' Ryan declares.

'Some kind of governmental agency conspiracy perhaps?' Peter questions.

'An undercover highly decrypted scientific experiment, but on what and for what?'

'Okay in which universe does that even make sense?' Caroline has squeezed her face tightly adding lines and contours in places she would never have known, unless she did it again in front of a mirror.

'Maybe not this one.' Peter points to some coordinates on the corner of the document.'

'Those aren't normal coordinates. There should be latitudes, longitudes and sometimes elevation. What's this extra figure?' Peter points to a series of numbers.

'Is that word sodomites?' Peter continues.

'I suppose the people doing the experiments are either gay or homophobic? Ryan remarks.

Caroline chortles. 'No silly, it's an old encryption system that was used in the Middle East. You see these random letters here.' Caroline points to a string of letters not making any sense. 'I'd imagine they're all encryptions of some sort.'

'The deciphering is done in reverse, with each letter corresponding to another letter in a parallel line of the alphabet. I might be able to decipher this, but it will take some time.' Caroline is excited.

'Wow, I'm impressed.' Ryan mutters.

'Thank you.' Caroline replies.

'What are these words?' Ryan points to the words "Panspermia." "Caesium." and "Grypania."

'Caesium is a radioactive element right?' Ryan checks with Peter.

They all gape at the screen as if seeing a laptop for the very first time.

'Done?' Caroline seeks permission to continue scrolling.

Both men nod their heads as if in a trance, the effort to speak is too much.

Caroline scrolls down the document and they're two lines running parallel with words in the middle.

'It looks Latin. Can you zoom in?' Peter checks with Caroline.

'I think so.' Caroline double clicks on the small image.

The words "popliteal fossa" is written diagonally in the middle of parallel lines. Next to this drawing is an object similar to a small transistor board. The kind you'll find in radios. Peter remembers playing with a circuit board when he was a young boy. You had to connect wires in different small springs and transistors to create a radio that transmitted genuine radio signals. The best creation was an International Morse Code which was a device used in communication between maritime vessels. It was a series of dots and dashes, with different series relating to a particular alphabet.

'Popliteal fossa…. what does that mean?' Peter instantly checks Google on his phone.

'It's the knee pit.' Peter immediately turns to Ryan.

Ryan begins lifting his trousers on his right leg. It's like he cannot lift the trousers up quick enough.

'What's going on?' Caroline is bemused.

'Hopefully nothing.' Peter snaps.

'I've been scratching my knee pit for a few days now, sometimes it itches like crazy. Can you see anything?' Ryan turns around so that Peter and Caroline can inspect behind his knee.

Chapter 21

Jaime wakes up on woodland floor; he spits leaf litter out of his mouth. He eventually realises where he is and hurriedly gets up looking around. He bends down to scratch his knee pit and scratches it for a while, it is one of those itches where you scratch and it just gets worse. He chafes his leg a while longer, then gives it a slap and ignores it. He scans around and tries to orientate himself. On his face is panic and concern.

In the distance about 300 yards are two men in wellies and hoodies watching closely. The men are like warped versions of Morecambe and Wise; they look like they just walked off a comedy set.

'Damn it, he's waking up.' The shorter of the men mutter under his breath, his voice sounding like that of a female.

'He can't be waking up, he mustn't leave that location.' The taller guy with a moustache gets up from his sitting position.

'What do we do?' The effeminate guy also gets up.

'We make sure he is back in that location.' The taller guy promptly walks in Jaime's direction.

Jaime spots both men in the corner of his eye but he pretends not to have seen them and walks faster away from them. Both men notice his change in pace and they also increase their pace.

Jaime continues to walk swiftly, the itch in his knee pit is becoming unbearable now, he forces his mind to ignore it and instead feels his pocket for his mobile phone, gets it out and speed dials whilst keeping the phone down close to his leg. He doesn't want to alert the hooded men to what he is doing.

'If you can hear me, please help. I'm in the woods and I think I'm in danger. I've woken up in the middle of nowhere and two weird men are after me.' Jaime talks down at the phone hoping that Lloyd has accepted the call.

'I think it might be the wood near the cemetery, please come now. Please, please hurry.' Jaime decides to leave the phone on and starts to walk in haste as he has seen in the corner of his eye that the men have increased their pace. He can't hear a voice from the phone and so there is no reason why the men would know what he is up to either. This gives him a morsel of comfort. He was always one to grasp at any positivity in a situation and this situation wasn't any different.

'D'ya think he's seen us?'

'He might have.' And with that the taller guy starts to run.

'Remember the spot!' He makes a photographic imprint of the area Jaime woke up in in his brain. He doesn't whisper anymore, but shouts as he believes Jaime has seen the both of them, and now they must catch him and bring him back to this spot. They only have a short time to do it in.

The both men have started to run towards Jaime and he puts the phone back in his pocket still not terminating the call and starts to run. The itch in his knee pit disappears as a result of the flush of adrenaline now coursing through his veins. He runs with all his might determined not to trip and fall as he jumps over the shrub in his path.

The taller man runs ahead of the shorter guy, but they are both slower than Jaime thanks to their chubby nature.

Jaime plummets through the wood like a deer, all the time hoping that his call went through and Lloyd was in fact on his way to his rescue. Who were those men? Why had he woken up in the middle of the wood? Had he been drugged? These thoughts flood through Jaime's cerebellum as he runs even faster gaining distance from the two weird men. He tries to remember what he was doing before waking up in the wood, and he recollects investigating quadrants, figures like coordinates in a book with the map of Clophill. What was the significance of these coordinates? What had he stumbled upon? He remembers feeling very welcomed by the locals, to begin with anyway, but afterwards people started to act shady. He had once observed how the village was so quiet on certain evenings, and then discovered everyone went to the town hall.

The taller man is now way ahead of the shorter man and he is struggling with his breath. Jaime is also gasping now and turns around to check and it appears he has lost them. He peers ahead and nothing is familiar, he has no idea in which direction he is running. He remembers his phone and gets it out to use the compass but now has to accept the gloomy realisation that his mobile has died. Perhaps he should have terminated the call and maybe he would have had some bars left on it. He scans around for somewhere to hide as he's out of breath now and it would be pointless running aimlessly not knowing in which direction he was going. For all he knew he could be running in a full circle right back into the hands of his pursuers. He spots bushes of cotoneaster and blackberry laden with fruit and he instantly finds this strange as he is sure they should not have fruit at this time of year. Nonetheless, something about the shrubbery draws him towards it and he runs in the direction of the shrub with his last reserve of strength. He checks to see if he has left any footprints and does not see any obvious marks. He makes sure he cannot see the two men in the distance and is relieved there is no sight of them.

He bends down near the shrub and starts to make his way into it, grasping the sleeves of his jumper with his hands and using the technique to move through the thorny bush. His face is left bare and he manages to get two substantial cuts on his face, one going all the way from his lower right cheek to his lower eyelid.

Jaime settles down in the shrub whilst nursing the cuts on his face with spit and his finger. He is confident no signs exist to show he has hidden in the shrub. He tries hard to think about his last memory before waking up in the woodland.

What were those coordinates and why marked on certain locations on the Clophill map? Why was it such a big deal and were these guys really trying to kill him?

The two men have now decreased their pace and are panting heavily. The taller guy is still ahead of the shorter guy.

'Donald is going to lose his mind if we don't get this chap and put him back in the spot.' The taller guy eyeballs the shorter man who is just catching up.

'What d'ya think he'll do with us?' The shorter guy struggles to get his words out as he's out of breath.

'I think it's best we don't think about it and just make sure we get him.' He checks the time on his watch.

Both men walk hurriedly in the direction they last saw Jaime running. After a while they start to run again having recovered from exhaustion. But this time they don't run as hard, they just keep a steady pace whilst paying severe attention to the woodland floor looking for any signs. The taller guy detects a patch of dead leaves on the snow dusted grass and can tell from inspecting them that weight has been applied on the leaves.

'This way.'

They both jog for a while, the taller guy occasionally changing course slightly when noticing something on the woodland floor or the way a small branch is bent slightly. Eventually the taller guy stops and sits down in damp cold leaf litter and listens. He listens intently.

The shorter guy eventually catches up and mimics him. They both sit catching their breath.

The taller guy scans the woodland for anything unusual, any mark that would give Jaime away. He gets up confidently.

'He is around here somewhere.' The tall guy pulls on his moustache.

'You sure?'

'Yes.'

Jaime can see the guys a few yards from him now and he tries to remain as still and quiet as a dormouse. The itch in his knee pit is so bad he cannot remember anytime where he had endured such an uncomfortable sensation on his skin. It is out of this world, he's never experienced anything like it. Is it because of the situation he's in that it's itching so bad and why? Why would his body let him down so badly? What was the point of adrenaline if it couldn't get rid of an itch? This was potentially a life and death situation and he must remain still as a statue, his life probably depended on it.

Jaime takes deep breaths in a meditative attempt to will the itch in his knee pit away but it doesn't work. He literally wants to cry in frustration as the itch is unbearable. A little tremor in the ground distracts him. Jaime continues to sit still watching the two men as they walk towards him. The taller guy appears to be studying the woodland and now and again stops and stares with the intensity similar to that of a cat on the hunt.

'He must be here somewhere.' The short guy mutters.

'He is.' The tall guy utters in confidence. 'Just come out mate, we won't hurt you and there is nowhere for you to run to anyway.'

Both men stand still listening earnestly.

Jaime is now crying partially from fear and partially from the itch in his knee pit which is now like prickling psoriasis. It's excruciating. He never knew skin irritation could be so bad. There is another slight tremor on the ground and he wonders what the vibration is. It's only a little tremor, nothing that should alert the two men after him.

'For fucks sake just come out! You aren't going anywhere and it's cold and you must be starving now.'

'Yes.' The effeminate guy agrees. 'You've been out here all night, it's cold, wet and miserable and you must want something to eat.' He regards his colleague with a sinister smile.

A crow caws in the distance and it lasts erringly too long.

Jaime cannot bear the itch anymore and reaches to scratch his knee pit as quietly as possible.

The tall guy hears the slight shuffle and scans the cotoneaster and blackberry bush with a stern eye. He observes the shrubbery in a disquieting fashion which causes the hair's on the back of Jaime's neck to stand to attention. Jaime's eyes widen in sheer terror. The tall guy now trudges towards him. Jaime is certain that the man can now see him.

The tall hooded man gets to the shrub and reaches for him but pulls his hand out just as quickly and curses as he picks thorns out of his palm. He takes a deep breath and tries again.

'Now, now, there's a good chap.' The guy with the moustache says. 'Come out and let's go get something to eat and get you warm.'

Jaime is now petrified. He is sure he is about to faint. His itch has disappeared. The tremor underneath him now intensifies. The tall guy's hand reaches for him and Jaime pulls back getting a thorn in his neck as he does so. The vibration increases and he can now hear a humming noise. The tall guy pulls his hand back to pay attention to his nose which is now dripping with blood. The shorter guy has his hands cupped over his ears. The humming is deafening now. All men are now on the floor. Jaime wonders why he is not bleeding from the nose and why he appears to be immune to the intense strange humming and vibration that has engulfed the area.

An intense humming pitch followed by a rippling flashing blur startles Jaime but does not harm him unlike his pursuers who now appear to be drying up before his very eyes. It's almost as if the water content in their bodies is being zapped out of them through osmosis. Whiteness engulfs Jaime's entire vision and the crescendo of the humming reaches a climax.

Jaime faints; it's all too much for his brain to compute. He later wakes up still in woodland albeit unfamiliar and he senses a dull itch in his knee pit. He slowly turns around and gasps as to the side of him are two dried up corpses.

Caroline and Peter scrutinise Ryan's knee with the torch from Caroline's smartphone.

'What can you see?' There is clear panic in Ryan's tone.

'It's like a rash but there appears to be a slit too to the side.' Peter stares intently at the soft depression behind Ryan's knee.

Caroline grabs her laptop and scrutinises the small circuit board on the screen that is next to the words popliteal fossa.

'It's the same size.' Caroline confirms.

'The same size as the transistor thing...... this is ridiculous. Just what exactly are we getting at here?' Peter tries to make sense of what is going on.

'Is there any way of getting it out?' Ryan grills still with panic in his voice.

'Not without a surgical knife, I don't think so.' Caroline's full attention is on the computer screen. She does her best to decipher the puzzle before her.

'Why....why would someone put an implant into anyone's leg and why Ryan's?'

Both Caroline and Peter look at each other and on that cue they start to raise their trousers too to check for a rash or itch that may have been numb for some reason. They turn around so that Ryan can look at both their knee pits.

'Don't see anything.' Ryan comments with a hint of disappointment.

'It's not itching as much, could that be good?' Ryan attempts to console himself.

'What else does it say in that document?' Peter moves in so that he can look too.

'Well, it looks like Clophill is marked for some reason. There are concentric circles in specific points on the map.' Caroline moves in closer to the map which she has now zoomed into.

'Isn't that where the road accident occurred?' She points to a circle on the screen. 'That is the A233 right?'

'I believe it is.' Ryan replies scanning the document as well. 'Is there anything else on the stick?' Ryan pulls his trouser leg down.

'Not that I can see, you would have thought something like this would be encrypted.' Caroline also pulls her trousers down over her knees.

'It does look very confidential, like something we shouldn't be seeing that's for sure.' Peter pulls down his trousers.

'I suggest we go to the hospital and see if they can perhaps x-ray your knee and ours for that matter, who knows. Then remove whatever they find and check it out.'

'You think that's a good idea?' Peter subconsciously touches his knee.

'If we do go to a hospital lets go to one away from this town - I think I'll be a lot more comfortable.'

'Yep good idea.' Caroline reaches for her car keys. 'I'll drive.'

'It's quite late now, we should go to A and E.'

'That's where I was going anyway.' Caroline grabs a coat, removes the USB stick from the laptop and put it in her pocket.

Chapter 22

Donald is sitting in his lounge listening to jazz. He inhales on a cigar, holds it and expels a bluish smoke. He blows it out of his mouth slowly admiring the volume of smoke he has exhaled. He reaches for a whiskey he has in a crystal glass and takes a gulp of it. Suddenly a ping comes from his laptop. He trudges over to the computer holding his neat whiskey close.

He sits down and stares at the screen which has only the word "CARELESS" on it. He puts the whiskey down almost spilling it as his hand is now shaking with nerves.

Donald grabs the mouse and starts to search his files on the computer. He opens one that reads "Clophill Finance" and another sub folder which reads "sdr."

The sound of children reverberates from Donald's workstation. He turns the volume down and carries on looking at the screen. He stares for a few minutes and deletes it and opens another subfolder called "sth." A little boy speaks to an older man, and sounds of moaning come out of the laptop. Donald clicks on another folder and another and another. He deletes them all, looking around him as he does so. His breathing now begins to return to normal. He comes out of that screen and stares at the word that has somehow attached itself to his screen saver. He stares at the word "CARELESS" again, and scratches his head. He turns the computer off. For some reason he's propelled to look at the windows to his lounge. Even though the curtains are all drawn he senses people are watching him. He stubs his cigar out and goes to sit down. He stares at the windows around his grey and white oval living room and contemplates. Now and then he peers across to his desk where the computer is, and he stares at it as if waiting for another ping. Perspiration forms on the brow of his forehead.

In another dimension which Donald is unaware of, morphing silhouettes are standing by the windows looking in at him. These frighteningly thin silhouettes steadily increase in numbers.

Donald finishes his cigar and gulps down the last of his whiskey. He gets up and heads towards the stairs to retire to bed but not before taking another quick glance at the computer on his desk. He stumps up the stairs carrying with him a dread that fills the pit of his stomach. He has always had this angst; he has learnt to live with it, albeit tonight's was a whole new 'shaker.' The whiskey will kick in soon enough and dissolve it as it always does. He will be asleep in no time he thinks to himself. Before reaching for his bedroom door he could swear that he hears the sound of children playing in a playground. It is late at night; no way will children be playing at this time of night. Has his computer switched itself back on? He wonders to himself but decides not to act on it. He is determined to get into bed and believes in the morning it will all be some bad dream. He gets into his bedroom and is used to the aroma of old farts and stale cigar smoke. He hurriedly takes off his clothes leaving his shorts on, and climbs into bed.

The next morning Donald wakes up and feels great. In fact, he cannot remember the last time he felt so great in the morning.

"How can this be, not even had my first cup of coffee."

He goes through his normal morning routine. Brushes his teeth and has a prolonged shower. He has never lingered in the shower and seldom had a bath; he just couldn't relax for that long. This time he enjoys the shower and is fully present to the water caressing his rotund body. He finishes showering and towels himself dry carelessly. He then strays to his bedroom, feeling as if he's walking on air. He can't believe how great he feels. He puts his clothes on, paying particular attention to his tie which he recently purchased from River Island. He peers in the full length mirror in the room and hardly recognises himself. He is smiling. He never smiles, definitely not in the mornings. He likes it and seeing himself smile makes him smile some more. He turns away from the mirror but not before giving his belly a tap with the palm of his hand.

In the kitchen he makes himself some porridge and sits down to eat it. He examines his kitchen as he eats. He always wanted a large kitchen; this one swung his decision on getting the house. He figured since he loved food so much he might as well have a house with a large kitchen. Hues of pine green and browns dominate the colour scheme and it certainly appears lived in albeit with a tad too much clutter. He has always lived with clutter. He finishes the last of his porridge, picks up his bowl and puts it in the dishwasher. He plods out to the car, gets in and drives, still retaining the smile on his face.

He drives to an elementary school and is instantaneously aroused. He parks his car and walks through huge gates. He can hear children playing in a playground a few yards away. His heart is racing with adrenaline as he reaches the playground. All the children are playing various kinds of games. Separate groups of boys and girls but occasionally the odd girl in a boy group and vice versa. He prowls in the midst of the children while attempting to conceal his erection by adjusting his trousers occasionally.

'You wouldn't have to fight on the other side.'

His mum whispers to him and it consoles him. He wonders briefly how come he can hear his mum whispering to him but he doesn't give it too much attention. He is aroused walking in the playground and feels like a pig in shit as he struggles to contain his excitement.

'You wouldn't have to fight on the other side.'

He hears his mum whisper again, it sounds so close, all around him. He could have sworn he felt hair brush his arm, it felt like tough fur but he carries on walking, going over to a particular corner where a little boy and girl hold hands and beckon to him to join them. The boy is mixed race and has tantalising hazel eyes whilst the girl is white with blond hair tied up in a bow on the top of her head. Her innocent blue eyes lure him towards them.

Donald is so excited he can hardly contain himself. He has spent all his life pushing this urge down, ignoring it, drinking it away and being a nasty person to himself and others just so he can punish himself for his perverse afflictions. Nonetheless, here he was with the universe somehow saying it was okay, setting him free to experience his perversions. For once, he allows his swollen penis to press against his jeans without any shame.

'There'll be no need for you to suppress it son.'

This time he looks around and feels ashamed as he could swear his mum is with him. He loses his erection hastily; his mum is nowhere to be seen. The young boy and girl continue to beckon him. They are backed up against a wall in a corner of the playground and they both look tantalizingly at him before they start to kiss.

Donald is aroused again and plods towards them. He feels fur on his arm again. This time he is sure it is fur but he sees nothing. The children caress each other and then something about the girl's hair stops him in his tracks. Her hair has moved at an awkward angle as the young boy caresses her. It is off centre on her head. The young girl turns to watch Donald just as her left eye starts to wink continuously. Her eyelid winks so fast it's now flickering. It flickers too fast to be human.

'You wouldn't have to fight on the other side. There'll be no need for you to suppress it son.'

Donald freezes on the spot now as he senses something is wrong. Something is wrong with where he is and what he is looking at. It's not real. The young boy now gazes at him and smiles. The smile is a bit too wide. It is fake and sinister; it's like the smile you'd expect from the puppet of a ventriloquist.

A sharp pain now shoots through his arm in the same position where he has been feeling tough fur. He inspects his arm and gapes at a huge gorge of flesh hanging off it. He is in shock as he witnesses the children's playground dissolve, and he now realises he's in a safari zoo with tigers. He looks around and hears people shouting for him to get back in his car, but it is too late, the tiger has gotten a taste of his blood. A couple of wardens rush towards him with stun guns shouting at the scene before them in an attempt to distract the tigers, and perhaps get some sense into the fat man who has driven into the park and chosen to get out of his car into tiger territory.

The tiger takes one keen look at Donald who stands paralysed with fear, blood pouring out of his arm. He attempts to figure out how he has gotten to the zoo. His whole morning was a sham. He should have known it was too good to be true. He never feels that great in the mornings. He remembers the word across his computer screen. "CARELESS" and that is the last thing his brain computes as the tiger now goes for his neck taking a huge bite. There is a lot of neck, but the tiger has a big jaw.

The stun gun is fired. Screams and shrieks fill the air from families in their vehicles around the park. Donald lies on his side, his neck like a fleshy faucet releasing red fluid. A sincere smile is plastered on his face as his mum's words resonate.

'You wouldn't have to fight on the other side.'

Chapter 23

'Did we not pass that building on the left?' Ryan tries his hardest not to scratch behind his knee.

"Perfect place to put a chip in you." He thinks to himself. "Your knee pit is completely concealed; even looking at it in a mirror proves difficult."

'I followed the map precisely.' Peter states with confusion in his voice.

'You should have let me drive.' Caroline says unconvincingly then stares out the window in a trance.

'What's up Caroline?' Peter touches Caroline's shoulder.

'Just remembering what was on the USB stick.'

They all wait awhile and then impatience gets the better of Ryan.

'Wanna let us in on what's going on up there?' Ryan checks his phone at the same time. He had sent a text to Teresa but had not got a reply. Teresa would always be his first point of comfort when he was stressed.

'This spot was marked on the map.' Caroline announces.

Peter stops the car abruptly in the middle of the country lane.

'Right Caroline spill, what are you getting at?'

'That building on the left.' She points to a decrepit building that appears misplaced. 'We've passed it already. This exact location was marked on the map we saw on this stick.' She holds the USB stick up.

Ryan laughs nervously.

'What are you saying that we're going around in circles? That we're somehow not able to get out of this damned town?'

In that precise moment a beep of a horn makes everyone in the car jump with fright.

'GET OFF THE ROAD WANKA!' Bellows from a driver in a speeding blue fiat. He avoids impact by driving on the grass verge.

Peter hastily puts the car into gear and moves the car into a convenient lay-by.

'C'mon what you're insinuating is ridiculous.' Peter puts the car into gear again and drives off taking a peek at the map on his lap. 'We must have taken the wrong turning that's all.'

Ryan checks his phone again and there's still no response from Teresa. He checks for a signal and there are a couple of bars. In seconds his signal disappears.

'Anyone else not got a signal on their phone?' There is alarm in Ryan's voice.

Caroline checks her pocket. 'No signal either.' She turns to Peter with concern.

'Can't reach my phone, it's in my back pocket.' Peter tries not to join in this crazy presupposition.

'Well lift up your butt and get it out.' Ryan is mixed with impatience and fear.

On cue a beep comes off his phone and Ryan hurriedly checks. A smile lights up his face as he reads the text and stares at the image of his little girl in a picture that has been sent by Teresa; tears well up in Ryan's eyes as he smiles at his phone.

Peter and Caroline watch Ryan and allow him the space to be in the moment with his daughter.

Peter pulls the car alongside a grass verge, climbing it to make enough room for other cars that may come through. He puts his head down on the steering wheel and inhales, filling his lungs to capacity before exhaling.

'It would appear we are going round in circles, no explanation and right now I'm pretty freaked out. Let's be grateful that we're in this together cause if I was on my own I would certainly crack up.' Peter's head is still on the steering wheel. Eventually he slowly lifts his head and turns around to look at Caroline then back at Ryan.

'This is fucked up.' Ryan retorts opening the car door and getting out. Behind his knee is not itching anymore and he is pleased for this plus. He walks over to the back of the car and leans on the boot looking around him.

Peter and Caroline also get out of the car and walk over to Ryan and do the same.

'There must be a rational reason behind all this…. I really hope so because this is too much.' Ryan exclaims looking at Caroline.

'I think it's time we called Contiana.' Peter suggests.

'Yep, you're right.' Ryan agrees as a car pulls up next to them and out gets Contiana.

'Hi, I think you need me.' Contiana walks towards them.

'How did you…don't worry.' Ryan mumbles.

'I think Jaime is back in this realm.' Contiana says looking at Peter.

'What, what do you mean?' Peter has on a more serious face than normal.

'I think he's back here with us, back in this reality.'

'Contiana you better be sure of what you're saying because I'm not sure I can cope with much more of whatever is going on around this fucked up town.' Peter walks up to Contiana.

'I'm certain, he is back with us.'

'How did he, how would he, how could he….' Peter wonders if it is shock that has impacted on his ability to construct a simple sentence together.

'I don't think it matters, how….where do we find him?' Ryan is much calmer.

'In the wood by the cemetery.' Contiana points in the direction which is north east of where they are.

'Any idea why we've been going around in a loop, even though we've followed a map?' Caroline reaches out her hand to shake Contiana's.

'Sorry…what?'

'We tried to get out of town and couldn't, we just kept going round in a circle, any idea why?'

'Really…..that happened?'

'Yes, I'm afraid so.' Peter tries to conceal a tear that has traced its way down his cheek.

'We ended up going past the same landmarks.' Ryan confirms, hoping it will alleviate the surprised tone in Contiana's voice.

'Wow, I've heard of that ability, I never knew it was actually doable.' Contiana mutters.

'Ability?' Caroline says the word like it's newly discovered vocabulary.

'Yes…. a very old spell of sorts that witches could do in the old days. I never knew it was still a practise, it's supposed to be ancient. I read up about it in some old manuscripts.'

'Okay so we're all under a spell?' Ryan is now in utter disbelief.

'Well, it doesn't quite work like that. it's not that you per se are under a spell, just that there is a spell on the boundary of the town.'

On cue the blue fiat that went past them earlier drives past them again, this time slower. A confused expression plastered on the driver's face.

Everyone turns to look at the blue fiat drive past.

'So in other words, no one can leave the town?' Caroline checks that she understands what she's hearing.

'At least it's not discriminatory.' Ryan utters.

'Where can I find Jaime? Where…how do I find him?' Peter stammers.

'Sorry, yes let's focus shall we.' Contiana rejoins.

'One good thing is that he won't be able to venture out of town, so that should make it relatively easy to find him.' Contiana adds.

'Your positivity has no bounds.' Ryan remarks with some sarcasm.

'It's put me in good stead.' Contiana replies with a smile.

'Please can we go now…. to the cemetery?' Peter does his best not to be dramatic and just drive or even run off on his own.

'Yes, Peter you come with me. Ryan, you and Caroline follow me. I think I may know the exact location by the cemetery. Contiana affirms then walks purposefully to her car.

Chapter 24

Jaime and Lloyd sit with their backs against a tree to the side of the one that was vomited on. Both of them have their hand on their tummy and caress it leisurely. Jaime smiles as he observes the puke that has escaped their guts.

'What's funny?' Lloyd pouts with disdain as he doesn't see anything funny about what's just happened to them.

'The difference in our sick.' Jaime points to the vomit down the bark and the one splattered on leaf litter on the ground.

'Different colours.' Lloyd manages to expel.

'Yep mine's darker and seedy from all the berries I've been having and yours is yellow; remnants of a more palatable diet.'

'Are you alright?'

'Yes...why?'

'Well, you're kinda acting strange.'

'Because I see the funny side of vomit?'

'Well, yes...we've just returned from another dimension, you were gone for god knows how long and...and we're here, alive, all in one piece it appears, apart from us throwing up, we appear fine, but who's to say we're not or don't become deluded?'

'You think I've lost my mind.' Jaime gets up off the ground.

'Well, it's not an everyday event to travel back and forth from different dimensions.' Lloyd also gets up.

'I guess I'm a little hysterical, but honestly I'm fine.' Jaime wipes leaf litter off his jeans. 'I need to get out of these clothes and get a decent wash.'

'I think there's a cemetery in that direction- that is our way out.' Lloyd declares with certainty.

Both men begin to walk with purpose north west of the wood.

Lloyd smells body odour on Jaime and wonders why he didn't smell it on the other side.

'Do you feel better?'

'I still feel a bit queasy but I'm fine, you?'

'Yea, I'm good.'

Both men continue to walk through the woodland. They both contemplate on recent events and decide to keep some of their thoughts to themselves. It was all crazy, a miracle that they even made it back. People would never believe them but both men were pleased that there was someone they could share their experience with....each other.

'Damn it.' Jaime scratches his knee pit on his left leg.

'What's wrong?'

'It's just a damn itch.' Jaime continues to scratch his knee pit.

'You probably got an insect bite or nettle sting.'

'It's quite intense, I give you that.' Jaime sits down on the woodland floor and pulls his trouser leg up to try and inspect where the flaring itch is coming from.

'Can you see anything?' He turns his leg around at an angle for Lloyd to inspect.

'It's sore...but, hang on a second.' Lloyd inspects further by kneeling down and bending in towards the knee pit. 'Is that a bite?'

'What is it?'

'It's like a slit on one side of where the rash has formed.'

'A slit?'

'Yea…like a small cut.'

'Does it hurt at all?' Lloyd presses down on the area of rash.

'Not particularly, it just itches like crazy…actually I remember it itching like mad before I went through the portal. The itch may have saved my life.'

'What are you talking about?'

'There were two men after me; I'm certain they were staying at the Inn. I think they may have been trying to kill me.'

'What makes you think that?'

'You remember all the stuff I was telling you before, well I may have opened a can of worms - there was some historical witchcraft information I stumbled on and there were sacrifices made using babies.'

'What?' Lloyd is not sure if this is the start of Jaime's delusion caused by dimension travel.

'It's all coming back to me now, I must have forgotten. There was some kind of witchcraft conspiracy in the town and…and a lot of people were aware of it. They were all in on it.' Jaime starts to panic and look around.

'What are you talking about?' Lloyd reaches for Jaime's shoulders. Jaime shimmies away.

'Listen, I'm not crazy. This village is cursed.'

'Okay, okay, I believe you, hell I came after you didn't I? Through alternate realities no less.'

'Why does my leg itch so badly?' Jaime starts to scratch again but this time with some annoyance.

'C'mon we better keep moving.'

'Yea you're right.' Jaime gets up and pulls his trouser leg down.

After both men get up they stand and stare in the distance. People are walking towards them. They are at least a mile away and they are at least twenty people all in wellies and waterproof gear, some of them are holding sticks. Jaime drops to the woodland floor instantly pulling Lloyd down with him.

'What the hell is going on?' Lloyd whispers.

'They know…. they know I'm back, they want to finish what the two men started, trust me stay down.' Jaime begins to panic.

'Right, you're scaring me now.'

'Good, you should be scared, you should be petrified and that's good.' Jaime declares whilst crawling to a nearby bush for cover. 'Follow me.'

Lloyd crawls after him, his heart racing so fast he thinks it might implode in his chest.

Behind the bush is a gully, both men allow themselves to roll into it, pulling branches and leaf litter around them to cover themselves.

A female voice calls out to get the attention of everyone.

'I know that voice.' Jaime whispers with a bit of hope but nonetheless stays put in the gully.

'Hey, what's going on?' Contiana bellows in the distance.

Both Peter and Ryan walk close to Contiana as they approach the crowd of people.

Lloyd starts to hum and stares into oblivion.

'Hey….hey.' Jaime hits Lloyd's arm. 'This is no time to zone out.'

'Sorry, sorry.' Lloyd lifts himself off the ground a little to peer over the gully and Jaime does the same.

The people have stopped approaching and instead are conversing with Contiana.

'I do know her, she's the.....'

'The white witch that lives in the wood.' Lloyd finishes Jaime's sentence for him.

'Do you think she knows?'

'Knows about what exactly?'

'Well, the whole parallel universe stuff.'

'Possibly...hopefully...who's the other two with her?'

'What other two?'

They're two men with her, standing to the side of her...on the left.'

'Oh my god, oh my god, it's Peter.'

'Sure.'

'Yes, I'm sure; I think I know my own boyfriend.' As soon as Jaime utters the words he realises there was no need for the sarcasm and wonders why he said it like that. He wonders if on some level he feels something for Lloyd. He did come after him after all, risking his life to do so. Well, he didn't ask him to, he thinks to himself and just then he knows why he's being that way. He does have feelings for Lloyd, feelings he will never show because he still loves Peter and there is no reason to end it with his partner because of some new found feelings for someone else. I'm with Peter and that's that.

'Do you think he knows we're here?'

'I don't see how he could possibly know but then again they are with Contiana.'

'This is true.' Lloyd continues to peer over the gully.

Jaime peeks at Lloyd through the corner of his eye. He tries to see if he can detect any hurt on his face. He loves Peter but he does not want to hurt Lloyd's feelings. That would be cruel and terribly ungrateful.

'What do you think Contiana is telling them?' Lloyd feels compelled to fill the silence.

'I don't really care so long as she distracts them long enough for them to forget what they were doing in the first place.'

'You seem certain they were coming for you.'

'That's because they were.' Jaime scoffs at Lloyd. 'Please believe me, there were two men who did not mean me well before I ended up in the other place.'

'I believe you….do we just stay here?'

'For now yes.'

Both men watch sternly and notice that Contiana gives one of the men in the group something. It's too far to see what it is she has just handed to one of the men. Jaime watches Peter and observes as he scans the wood and he smiles to himself. He can see worry in Peter's eyes even from that distance and he feels his love and allows it to flow over him.

Eventually the people begin to disperse and both Lloyd and Jaime breathe a sigh of relief. They continue to watch cautiously though just in case and the people all leave apart from Contiana, Peter and Ryan. The three of them begin to walk towards the gully where the two men are still cautiously peering over.

'It should be safe now.' Lloyd starts to get up.

'Hang on...hang on a minute, let's at least wait until the other people are out of sight first.' Jaime pulls Lloyd back down. Both men stay put and continue to watch.

'Psst.'

Both men look behind them and can hardly believe their eyes. In the gully next to them also on all fours are Contiana, Peter, Caroline and Ryan.

'It's an old witch's trick. Do not believe what you see. This is Caroline and Ryan by the way.' Contiana points to Ryan and Caroline.

Both men look back around to witness the other Contiana, Peter and Ryan still walking leisurely towards them.

'How, how....how can this be?' Lloyd stutters.

'You need to follow us.' Contiana commands.

'God Jaime I thought you were dead, I'm so glad you're alive.' Peter whispers with tears in his eyes.

'Hang on a second, how do we know YOU'RE the real ones?' Lloyd cross examines.

Jaime scrutinises the other three approaching them, albeit still some distance way. He was taken aback by the sadness he thought he saw in Peter's eyes. Did he just imagine it? Was it some ill founded desperation to see just what he wanted to rather than what was really there? He stares back at the Peter and Contiana and the other two in the gully with them, and he stares into Peter's eyes.

'Jaime it's me.' Peter is hurt. 'The three people coming towards us are complete strangers, what exactly are you seeing?'

Both Lloyd and Jaime are breathing heavily. It's all too weird.

'Prove it. Can they prove it? Can Peter prove it is him?' Lloyd checks for approval from Jamie.

Jaime continues to look at Peter trying desperately to see if he is genuine or not, if he isn't, the likeness is uncanny.

'How...why would they mimic three of you? Why not...Caroline too?' Lloyd whispers with some force.

'What?' Ryan is now feeling irritated.

'Why would they mimic the three, why not just mimic Peter if it's about luring Jaime out?' Lloyd cross examines.

'I don't….for crying out loud we need to get out of here now, and we're the real people who've been through hell to get here.' Ryan speaks with anger and a bad feeling in his gut. Ryan has a powerful bout of déjà vu and for some reason remembers what his little girl said to him on the phone.

'I know somewhere, some other place you and mummy and me are together.'

Ryan always developed a sense of peace whenever he experienced déjà vu as he believed when he had this phenomenon it meant he was exactly on the right path, exactly where he was meant to be in life. In this situation he was not sure, he certainly did not feel peace. He may very well be killed and the whole situation was weird beyond belief so why déjà vu now and what did his daughter mean by those words. How can something so profound come out of his daughters mouth?

'I guess they know that three of us are looking for you. They may not know of Caroline.' Peter contends calmly.

'Listen Jaime it's me. Peter whispers with more urgency and gets his wallet out of his pocket. He gets out the sticker that was left by Jaime in their bathroom with the words: "To Peter, my better half - flush the goddamn toilet! Love always Jaime." He shows it to Jaime. 'I've been carrying this with me, ever since, have no idea why, I guess it cheers me up when I read it.' A tear wells up in Peter's left eye, the eye that always starts to shed a tear, which Jaime is all too familiar with.

Jaime crawls up to Peter and both men embrace each other with as much affection as they can given the situation they're in.

'Can we please get out of here now?' Ryan questions in desperation.

'I can't believe it.' Jaime gapes at the other three people walking towards them. Except now they aren't Peter, Ryan and Contiana, they are complete strangers.

'People projecting...yet another old witch's trick. I have a feeling it isn't just parallel universes that are being opened, these tricks are all from ancient times.' Contiana declares scrambling out of the gully to find yet another cover.

'They would have had to have tested this.' Contiana remarks.

'What do you mean?' Peter asks befuddled.

'In order for it to work successfully; it must have been tested on at least one of the reciprocating copy-humans, so to speak.'

'How exactly would that test be carried out, do you know?'

'Did you have an experience of seeing people…and in the next instant the people were different?' Contiana is stoic.

Peter remembers seeing the guys at the Inn's reception and then Ryan seeing girls in the same reception minutes later.

'I think I did yes, at the Inn I'm staying at. They were two men and then literally a couple of minutes later Ryan reported they were ladies. I checked and indeed they were two ladies. It happened twice and the swap was too quick to make any sense.'

'This is much more dangerous than I originally envisioned…please follow me.' Contiana's serious face unsettles Ryan and Peter.

Contiana leads the way, still on all fours but somehow moving swiftly, like how a chimpanzee would move. The others follow, keeping as low down as possible. They crawl quickly all the way to another bank and then Contiana signals that they all get up.

'How is this possible?' Caroline pinches herself discreetly.

'Trust me anything is possible with what Lloyd and I have been through.' Jaime embraces Peter properly.

'Missed you so much.'

'Me too, I never gave up hope.' Peter holds Jaime tight.

Lloyd considers them with a smile smeared with a hint of jealousy but overall is pleased for the both of them. "Gay people do have it rough; with societal pressures and prejudices from living in a heterosexual world. Constant bombardment from adverts and media which insinuate gay people are second rate citizens somehow. It was a miracle that any gay couple survived. Ultimately though, love ruled."

A little further and the group arrive at two parked vehicles.

'Let's all head back to mine, we need to conclude this now, we can't hesitate.' Contiana asserts.

'Have you got wifi?' Caroline holds up the USB stick.

'I do indeed, I may be a hippie witch but I'm with the times.' Contiana winks at Caroline.

Ryan, Peter and Jaime get in the car with Contiana whilst Lloyd gets in Caroline's car.

Chapter 25

The party of people looking for Jaime in the woodland stop suddenly in their tracks. They look at each other as if in a trance, and they all take a few steps backwards before standing still again. They look at each other with complete surprise in their faces.

In another dimension, morphing silhouettes surround and watch the now confused congregation closely.

There is a slight tremor on the ground but the people are unaware, they continue to stare at each other with confusion, but do not utter a word. The tremor on the ground continues like a small earthquake, and then there is a blinding light that happens to be brighter than daylight. Everyone puts their hands up to cover their eyes, still not uttering a word. The tremor intensifies and a humming sound ensues. The light brightens some more and flashes out, it's likened to the coda of a sparkler or fire work. The tremor stops simultaneously and deadening silence envelopes the wood. It's as if even the wildlife are perturbed with the strange phenomenon.

The people slowly take their hands away from their faces and again look around at each other. Eventually a few of them attempt to say something and incoherent noises come out of their mouths. The locals discover to their horror that they are unable to speak. There is complete mayhem and although a terrifying experience to everyone involved, to the others looking in from the other dimension it is comedic as various sounds are expelled which do not make any sense at all. As the people realise they're not making sense they try harder to communicate, making more alarming but still incoherent noises. It is like a replay of the tower of Babel.

The morphing thin silhouettes look on and eventually they vanish, the people in the woods never realising their existence.

Everyone sits in Contiana's kitchen, candles all ablaze. The radio is on and creates good background noise. Contiana does not remember ever having so many people in her home. She is delighted, although living like a recluse she does love people mostly and appreciates having the company.

'You sure we're safe here after last time?' Ryan fidgets in his chair.

'Oh yes… yes, I think it's all over.' Contiana puts drinks on the table.

'All over?' Peter also fidgets.

'They're still so many unanswered questions.' Caroline waves the USB stick and then plugs it into her laptop.

'Well, I think we can find all the answers safely here with no danger to us, thanks to Jaime.' Contiana glances at Jaime and smiles.

'Oh, what do you mean?' Jaime scratches his knee pit.

'You have an unbearable itch in your knee pit too?' Ryan looks at the others and then at Jaime.

'I do it was itching before I ended up in the...the other place and then now it's flared up again although nowhere as bad.' Jaime touches behind his knee.

'Yea mine too, it was itching like crazy before but now it's subsided.'

'What are you referring to?' Contiana probes.

'We believe some kind of electronic device has been implanted in their knee pits.' Caroline spins her laptop around so Contiana can see the image of a small device amongst other weird symbols and letters all scattered across the map of Clophill.

'Fascinating.' Contiana scans the document downloaded from the USB stick.

'Let me see your knee pits.' Contiana beckons to both men to come over to her. She inspects both men's legs meticulously.

'I should be able to remove whatever it is you have in there, I was a nurse in a former life.'

'Really?' Ryan is genuinely surprised.

'Yes really, you'll both need to take turns on my table. 'Contiana gets up and saunters over to a corner of her kitchen and pulls out a massage table.

Lloyd and Caroline are engrossed in deciphering the document on the laptop.

'Jaime you get on first.' Contiana beckons.

Jaime and Peter get up and walk over to the massage table and Jaime gets up on it, lies on his front and rests his face in the padded hole. Peter gets underneath the table, sits on the floor, meets Jaime's eyes and gives him a kiss on the lips.

'You okay?' Peter traces his finger along a scar on Jaime's face.

'Yes, I'm fine thanks and you?'

'I'm good.......I'm really good.' Peter kisses him again on the mouth and then kisses his forehead and eyes.

'I'm going to combine medicines here, western and eastern, so bear with me.' Contiana rubs herbal ointment on Jaime's leg then administers an injection.

'You shouldn't feel anything.' Contiana reassures whilst getting a small scalpel out of a satchel.

'Just look at me.' Peter holds Jaime's shoulders firmly.

'People were used as test subjects.' Lloyd stares at the laptop. 'These coordinates are all wrong but they have the real coordinates in there too.' Lloyd points to the coordinates in the document.

'See these symbols here.' Lloyd points to the ☐ and Y. 'These symbols were scattered in certain areas of the wood, they mean something and I think they're important spots in the geography of the wood where portals to other dimensions are opened.'

'Right….Lloyd you work on those symbols whilst I try to decipher these random letters.' Caroline draws lines on a piece of paper and writes the alphabet and then another string of letters known as a cipher string. She starts to draw lines from one alphabet to another until she finally comes up with a word but she is not sure that she makes sense of it.

"MICCAN"

'Does this make sense to you?' Caroline shows Lloyd the word.

On the massage table Contiana is working her magic. Jaime is now unconscious as Contiana uses the scalpel to delicately cut an area in his knee pit. Jaime is only aware of the background noise coming from the radio. Peter gets up off the floor and stands next to the table taking Jaime's hand in his. Contiana starts to pull on the object in Jaime's knee pit. She mindfully removes it and places it on a dish by the side of her. Peter glimpses at it, then at Contiana.

'We'll look into that later let me make sure this cut is sterilised.' Contiana begins to dab Jaime's leg with a cotton bud.

'So what did you mean earlier when you said we're safe thanks to Jaime?' Peter admires his boyfriend as Contiana nurses him.

'Excuse me.' Contiana focuses on Jaime's knee.

'You kinda said it was all over thanks to Jaime....what did you mean by that?'

'Oh...Not sure how to tell you this but Jaime was a male witch in a former life. I figured this out when he first came to see me. I believe he still harnesses certain powers without knowing.'

'What...what are you talking about?'

'MICCAN...does that make sense to you guys?' Caroline interrupts.

Everyone looks up at Caroline and Lloyd with blank faces and eventually return to what they are doing.

'I think there may be another encryption we're not seeing.' Lloyd turns away from the symbols for a second.

'See this here.' Lloyd shows Caroline a selection of capital letters reversed. 'Notice how all these letters are reversed except the letter A.' Lloyd continues.

'What do you think that means?' Caroline continues to stare at the word.

'WICCAN!' Lloyd shouts.

'Oh my god, you're right…all the letters reversed except the letter A.'

Lloyd smiles to himself.

'I'm still none the wiser though…what does Wiccan mean?' This time Caroline takes her eyes off the word.

'Male witch.' Contiana claims looking at Lloyd and Peter.

'I thought a male witch was a warlock.' Lloyd retorts.

'Yes true and the term warlock in its original Scottish translation is a Wiccan or male witch.' Contiana affirms.

'And Jaime is a…a Wiccan?' Peter stammers.

'Yes he is but not only that, he is one with exceptional emotional intelligence.' Contiana adds.

'And you think that this had something to do with his ability to go through the dimensional portal and indeed get back and stop any further peril to us?' Peter checks on Jaime who is still unconscious. 'How exactly is that possible?'

'We have another word….HANNAH, any ideas why we have WICCAN and HANNAH alongside symbols and coordinates?' Caroline plays with her upper lip.

'Hannah…wasn't that the name of your friend?' Ryan stares at Contiana.

'Yes…Hannah Coleman.'

'Was she also a witch?'

'Yes…sheeeeee was but not just any kind of witch, let me see that document.' Contiana picks up the tiny object she has removed from Jaime's leg and walks over to where Lloyd and Caroline are sat scrutinizing the laptop. She pulls up a chair and sits in front of the laptop staring at the inscrutable document.

'These symbols look ancient, and this is supposed to be the thing I removed from Jaime's leg?' Contiana points to a diagram on the electronic notes.

'Yes it is and I would really like it if the one in my leg was removed too…soon.' Ryan grimaces.

Contiana inspects the object which is similar to an electronic chip and scrutinizes the diagram on the laptop screen.

'It looks vastly advanced but I think it's some kind of tracker, the question is why and who would put this into someone?' Lloyd is alarmed.

Ryan paces up and down, fidgeting and picking at his fingers. 'Please can we start on my leg?' He retorts.

'Sure, sure, let's get Jaime up.' Contiana gets up. 'Keep a good hold of that.' She gives the object to Lloyd.

Peter starts to gently shake Jaime's shoulder. Jaime stirs a little and opens his eyes and smiles as soon as he sees Peter's face.

'Whatever was in your leg is now out.' Peter reassures.

'That's good, I feel really drowsy.'

'You need to lie down and rest.' Contiana commands, walking up to Jaime.

Ryan follows behind Contiana and does not hesitate to get on the top of the massage table as soon as Jaime is off. He places his head in the headrest with the opening and stares at the floor.

'These coordinates are not right, they're like nothing I've ever seen and I am good with this kind of stuff. Dare I say it…they…just don't belong.'

Everyone stares at Lloyd not saying anything for a few seconds.

On the radio there is a breaking news bulletin. The newsreader announces there has been a gruesome death in the safari zoo not far from Clophill. The victim is Donald, the mayor of Clophill. Everyone is in shock.

"His enormity must have caught up with him." Caroline thinks to herself.

Contiana turns up the volume on the radio.

"Also breaking news - a group of people have returned from woodland not being able to speak. They are being closely monitored in the local hospital as there is no explanation to the strange phenomenon. No one is sure why they were in the woodland in the first place. It was only a short while ago they were in the town hall when they had to evacuate because blackbirds were crashing into the building."

Everyone looks at one another for a few seconds until Ryan breaks the silence, mainly to ensure he can still speak but also to encourage a move on with getting the strange device out of his leg. He stays head down on the massage table staring at the floor whilst he says.

'This is all sounding and looking more sinister by the second and I'm sure we're all in shock by the unusual events. However, I would be particularly grateful if this thing from my leg is removed.' Ryan raises his tone towards the end of the sentence for emphasis. He is not as self conscious as no one can see the glowering expression on his face.

'Right oh, scalpel and alcohol please Peter.' Contiana asserts.

Ryan's trouser leg is lifted and his knee pit dabbed with alcohol and some of the herb mixture, then Contiana administers the injection.

'Right stay still Ryan, you should start to feel drowsy but you shouldn't feel any pain, in awhile I'm going to remove the object okey-dokey.' Contiana tries to comfort him.

Contiana starts to cut at Ryan's knee pit with as much delicacy and attention likened to the Chinese creating art on a grain of rice. She takes a pair of tweezers and starts to pull at the small object.

Interference bounces off the radio and laptop screen and everyone looks up at each other.

'Ow...Ow arghh owwwww that hurts!' Ryan bellows.

Contiana freezes for a second before desperately trying to pull out the object.

'Shouldn't he be out by now?'

Contiana does not reply but continues to tug at the object.

'Hold him down will you.' Contiana commands.

Peter holds him down.

Lloyd hits save on the laptop and takes the USB stick out and walks over with Caroline to assist Contiana.

'God damn it!' Ryan shouts.

The interference on the radio and laptop continues.

Contiana manages to get the object out of Ryan's leg just before Ryan passes out. She drops the item and tweezers on the table. 'I'm sure I was getting an electric current from that thing.'

'Really…like an electric shock?' Caroline realises the stupidity of her question.

'Yes, pretty much.'

The interference continues for a few more seconds before stopping. The radio and laptop frequencies return to normal.

'What was that all about?' Peter stares at his slack-jawed colleagues.

'God knows.' Contiana utters.

'Is Ryan okay?' Caroline asks.

Contiana checks his vitals. 'His pulse is very weak; I think we may need to call an ambulance just to be on the safe side.' Contiana says.

Caroline starts to phone for an ambulance.

Peter goes to Ryan who is lying still on the massage table and puts his hand on his shoulder. 'You'll be just fine buddy.'

Jaime strolls up to Peter and holds his hand.

'So why do you think we have HANNAH and WICCAN in a document filled with symbols and weird coordinates?' Caroline sits back down next to the laptop. Lloyd has put the USB stick back in.

'You really think the coordinates are not right?' Caroline mutters.

'I do and like I said I know a couple of those coordinates are where there was a dimensional portal.'

Caroline scratches her head.

'Just how were the witches in the old days able to figure out that a child will become evil?' Caroline watches Contiana with fascination as she pampers over Ryan on the table.

'They were able to distort reality somehow and see into the future.'

'By going into a dimensional portal unscathed.' Lloyd's tone is likened to a Eureka moment. 'People needed the witches to understand the portals - I believe they were experimenting...using us. The phenomenon at Clophill is unique, that perhaps doesn't have a reason but this document leads me to believe people are experimenting on others to understand the portals. That will explain the tracker implanted in Jaime and Ryan's knee, the ancient coding and deciphering system and the sheer craziness of this town.' Lloyd mentions without taking a breath.

'The witches had to be special - extra sensitive like you said, more emotional intelligence, and Hannah and Jaime were the key.' Lloyd adds.

'That would mean….me coming here to research witchcraft was predestined somehow.' Jaime glances at Peter.

'It would explain how you were able to figure out a way of getting back from the other side. I don't think I would've ever figured it out even though I was able to get in.' Lloyd confesses.

'Do you feel different or have any inclination that you may have something weird going on for you?' Peter realises his words are all jumbled.

'That made sense.' Jaime teases.

'In the other dimension, although I was terrified, more frightened than I've ever been in my life actually, I did somehow know I'd be fine…...Looking back now, I just did. There was something quite weird…. the men that were chasing me were by my side in the other dimension as dried up corpses. There was no explanation; it was if all their water had been diffused out of them.'

'There was something in the document about oxygen and hydrogen being one of the most combustible friendly elements. I didn't pay much attention to it then cause there was other weirder stuff to contemplate.' Lloyd recalls.

'Water...hydrogen and oxygen; the tear in the universe causes the elements to combust and being as humans are mostly water...wow, but why some people and not others?' Peter cross-questions.

'We already ascertained that; although witches can also be combusted in the right conditions. The folklore of witches being annihilated with water comes from this fact.' Contiana utters matter-of-factly.

'I guess that explains that.' Jaime adds.

The sound of a siren resonates in the distance and Contiana checks on Ryan one last time by touching his forehead.

'We better get him set and we probably best think of what we're going to say.' Contiana regards the people in her home whom she has grown so fond of in such a short time.

'Oh yea....we could say he had an accident in the woods, they don't need to know more.' Peter mentions holding Ryan's hand.

'Yep that sounds great to me.' Caroline checks with Lloyd for affirmation.

'Yea, alright.' Lloyd mutters.

Chapter 26

Ryan can hear sounds of people and various equipment around him and he can feel the bed beneath him. He eventually realises that he is lying in a hospital bed and whilst he is conscious he decides not to open his eyes but instead listen to the sounds around him and reminisce about the events he's experienced in the last few days. He remembers lying on the massage table waiting for Contiana to remove the foreign object from his knee pit. He thinks about the events and how weird it has all been. People missing, witches, parallel universes; for a second he wonders whether it has all just been a dream but he knows in his heart of hearts that that is not the case at all. It has all been very real indeed, but it had ended well. Peter had found his partner and they were reunited and that was the main objective, to hell with all the whys?

As he lies there deciding not to open his eyes he hears the sound of his little girl and that changes his mind instantly. He opens his eyes and is immediately blinded by the bright light in the hospital. "Why do hospitals lights have to be so bright?"

He winces and tries to focus and he sees his daughter running towards him.

'Daddy!' Chloe runs up to her dad and falls into his embrace. Teresa walks behind with a smile on her face.

'How you doing buddy?' Teresa touches Ryan's forehead.

'I'm fine; thanks so much for coming….. you didn't have to.' Ryan continues to hug Chloe tightly.

'Don't be daft.' Teresa reaches out to hold his hand.

'What happened anyway….was told you reacted badly to a combination of anaesthetics?' Teresa continues to hold his hand.

'It would seem so, it's a long story. Someone was helping me remove some strange device that had been implanted in my leg.'

'Was this person a doctor?'

'Yes….well she had been a nurse.'

'And what do you mean by strange device?'

'I will tell you all…I promise (coughs), I need some water.'

Teresa grabs the glass that is by his bedside and fills it up with water from a jug also by his side. Chloe sits up on the bed next to her dad. Ryan takes the glass and drinks the water like someone parched.

'You okay daddy?'

'Yes I am baby girl, I'm just fine.' Ryan puts the glass down and gives her another hug.

Contiana, Peter and Jaime walk towards the ward that Ryan is in. Ryan spots them and breathes air of relief.

'Great, these guys should be able to explain exactly what happened.'

Teresa observes the three people walking towards them and instantaneously warms to Contiana. She has always been drawn to hippies or people that come across as a hippie.

'How you doing matey?' Peter is sure he is within auditory distance.

'Hey, I'm okay…..Thanks.'

Peter stops dead in his tracks as Chloe turns around to look at him.

She is the girl that he saw on the street in Clophill, the one that whispered to him and then disappeared after being distracted by a noisy truck.

'**There are other beings.**' The words now resound in Peter's head.

"How is this possible? Why did I see this little girl in some weird vision? There are other beings. What does that mean?"

'Children often sense alternate realities. But on top of this some children are extra sensitive and will have a spiritual doppelganger…… a kind of replica that guides people.'

'What's up Peter?' Concern resonates in Jaime's voice.

'Oh nothing…… nothing, just thought of something.'

'How are you doing Ryan?' Peter tries desperately to shake off what he has just experienced. There is a time and place for disclosing such insane happenings and here and now wasn't the place. He will have to wait to speak to the group without alarming the little girl and her mum.

'I'm fine…. you sure you're alright?' Ryan holds his daughter's hand.

'Yea, yea I'm fine, just thought of something that's all…will tell you later.'

Whimpering, screaming and other vocal oddities emit from a corridor with compartments for single beds and one to one areas. Consultants and other professionals discuss in a meeting about the lack of understanding to what happened to some of the Clophill locals when they returned from a nearby woodland.

'It makes no sense; none of them had any medical history that would explain the sudden mental breakdown.' One lady in a lab coat mentions scanning an electronic tablet.

'Could there have been some kind of gas leak we're not aware of that has affected their brains?' Another man in a lab coat mutters. He's wearing glasses that are propped way down his nose and look like they could fall off any minute.

'God knows, what do we do? Wait to start getting sightings of woodland animals exhibiting neurological abnormalities?'

'It's all completely bonkers.' Another man exclaims. He has dreadlocks and is wearing trainers with his white doctors overall.

'Well, we keep monitoring until we get some answers. Maybe we can get some meaning in their gibbering.' The lady with the tablet now looks up at her colleagues with the same perplexed face as theirs.

Along the corridor some of the patients are sitting down and rocking; while some are strapped to a bed shaking. Everyone is speaking words which sound like gobbledegook to the doctors.

'We shouldn't have killed the babies, we shouldn't have; even though we knew their future, we shouldn't have...we shouldn't have!' A lady shouts whilst shaking violently in her strapped bed.

'Need to keep testing, need to keep testing, need to keep testing, need to keep testing.' A man staring out of an immense rectangular window repeatedly mutters to himself.

'Found the tracker, found the tracker, found the tracker, found the tracker, found the tracker.' Another man repeats whilst slapping the back of his knees.

'Now they know, now they know, now they know, now they know.' Another man repeats rocking back and forth in his chair.

'Upset the slender ones. Now we must pay.' Another whispers and stares out of the same rectangular window.

'All okay on the other side, all okay on the other side, all okay on the other side.' One man chants smiling whilst rocking back and forth in his chair.

The shadowy figures are looking in from the other side of the rectangular window. There are hundreds of them. Their heads turn from side to side occasionally as if having a telepathic conversation.

One of the doctors looks through the window which a couple of patients are staring through and sees nothing but a yellow field covered in rapeseed plants. He observes the man rocking in his chair and goes to touch him and the man flinches albeit still smiling. The man continues his rant about the other side.

Dramatically, all the patients suddenly go quiet and turn to look at the vast window.

'I think you guys better get out here!' The doctor standing in the corridor shouts for all the other doctors in the meeting room, who all come running out.

'Going now, going now, going now, going now, going now.' All the patients start chanting hysterically. Some are crying loudly whilst others sob quietly.

The doctors stand dumbfounded staring at the patients.

The shadowy figures now stop turning their heads from side to side and stand perfectly still. A blinding bright flash which only the patients can see, burns through the atmosphere and when it finally subsides, the shadowy thin figures are gone.

Epilogue

A little girl plays in a sandpit in a deserted children's playground in a park. She smiles and has sparkle in her eyes; she is lost in her rich imagination as an only child often can be. She hums as she plays in the pit; drawing in the sand with her finger and then rubbing it out and drawing again.

A couple sitting on a bench a few yards away pay close attention to her.

'Joanne.' The mother calls out to her child.

The little girl turns around and she is the spitting image of Chloe.

'Yes mummy.'

'Turn around honey so mummy can take a picture of you, you look so beautiful.'

The little girl turns around as instructed.

The mum takes a picture.

A man walks up to the couple.

'Mr and Mrs Faber?'

'Yes.' The little girl's father responds. Both parents turn around and the dad is the spitting image of Ryan while the mum is the spitting image of Teresa.

'Hi, I'm Stephen, Joanne's teacher.' The man puts out his hand to shake the father's hand.

Stephen isn't just handsome but has one of those faces that's easy and pleasing on the eye.

'I was going to invite you both to the school to talk about Joanne.'

'Oh...is everything okay?' The mum has concern in her voice.

'Oh, yes....yes everything is fine, just wanted to talk about Joanne's exceptional imagination. I think she might be gifted and wanted to see what your thoughts were on it. I think she might very well benefit from having her imagination honed.'

'Oh, well she enjoys her own company so I guess you have to be good at making up mental pictures, especially at her age.'

'Yes…but there is so much more.'

The little girl continues to draw in the sand, still humming as she does so. She has drawn symbols of some kind. ⳨ and Y. She peeks out the corner of her eye and watches her parents discuss with her teacher. She smiles to herself. It is an all knowing smile. She rubs out the symbols she has drawn in the sand and gets up to walk towards her parents and teacher.

The Faber family sit at the table eating breakfast. The kitchen has an old style country cottage feel. However, there is an expensive tall fridge freezer which dispenses ice cubes, crushed ice and cold water. This is out of place in the kitchen. On the fridge door are several pictures attached with various fancy fridge magnets. One of the pictures is the one taken of Joanne in the sand pit. On looking closely there appears to be a symbol camouflaged in a hedge in the background of the picture. Strangely one part of the hedge is laden with fruit, whilst the other part is barren. The symbol looks like ᴆ.

Printed in Great Britain
by Amazon